First published in Great Britain by Scribo MMXI,
Scribo, a division of Book House, an imprint of
The Salariya Book Company
25 Marlborough Place, Brighton, BN1 1UB
www.salariya.com

Text Copyright © Alex Woolf MMIII
ISBN 978-1-907184-55-0
The right of Alex Woolf to be identified as the author of this work has been asserted
in accordance with sections 77 and 78 of the Copyright, Designs
and Patents Act, 1988.

Book Design by David Salariya

© The Salariya Book Company
& Bailey Publishing Associates MMXI

Printed and bound in Dubai

The text for this book is set in Cochin
The display types are set in Nikona X1

CHRONOSPHERE

Book 1

Time out of Time

Alex Woolf

A division of Book House

CONTENTS

CHAPTER ONE

CHILDHOOD'S END

"Who shall hold it, and fix it, that it be settled awhile, and awhile catch the glory of that everfixed Eternity… Who shall hold the heart of man, that it may stand still…?"

Augustine, Confessions, Book XI, Section XI, Paragraph 13

Time was not on Raffi Delgado's side. Through droplets of sweat and his dirt-smeared visor, he could glimpse the finish line – a horizontal sword of light that shimmered in the haze up ahead. In his reflectors loomed the maroon bulk of Red Oakes' hoverbike, steadily gaining on him with the passage of every second. Raffi knew he wasn't going to make it. He'd expended too much supercondenser power in the early stages of the race. Now his hoverbike's ionic fluid propulsors were weakening. As Red began to pull alongside him, Raffi could see the boy's triumphant grin beneath the dome of his helmet. Red was probably already imagining himself on the podium, fist clenched in victory. He would brag about this for months. It would prove that on the biggest stage – the final of the Paridex Annual Under-18 Hoverbike Championships – Red Oakes was the best.

Trouble was, it simply wasn't true. Red was a spoiled rich kid from Channel Island City in Central Londaris. Any modest talent he may have been born with had been artificially augmented out of all recognition by technologies that only his super-rich parents could afford – neural implants, weight and muscle control systems, reflex accelerators, balance correctors and other such bionic enhancements. Raffi, by contrast, hailed from the humble northern outlands of Londaris Megacity. He'd bought his first hoverbike only three years ago, and was still paying it off. He was a 'natural', unaugmented by any drug, implant or prosthesis, and he'd reached this final through sheer determination and raw, untutored skill. Tomorrow was his 18th birthday, after which he would be forced to leave behind the world of hoverbike racing for good. This was his last and only chance to show the world who he was.

With sickening inevitability, Red began to pull into the lead. There were less than 300 metres to go now. Raffi could sense the excitement rippling through the finish-line crowd. Red was their favourite. Raffi's year-long dream would shortly evaporate in the explosion of cheers for his rival. He already had his throttle open to the max, and could almost hear the ion clouds bombarding the air molecules in his bike's accelerating unit, producing its diminishing supplies of thrust – there was nothing more he could do.

Or was there?

If he couldn't increase his power, perhaps he could decrease his weight or drag. He recalled his mother's early birthday present, given to him that morning: a St Christopher medallion, which he'd attached to the tailguard behind his seat. He remembered the surprising heaviness of it – its loss might make a small difference, not a lot, but maybe just enough. Raffi reached behind him with his left hand, feeling with his gloved fingers for the tie. Carefully, he loosened the knot, then felt it quickly unravel as the slipstream took hold of the medallion and whipped it into the bike's downdraft. The resulting surge of unencumbered power took him abreast of Red, then very slightly ahead of him. Red's grin fell into a gape of astonishment. The crowd's expectant cheers turned to puzzled murmurs. Raffi knew he'd only made the tiniest difference – no more than a few metres per second – Red's superior power would make up the gap in no time at all. But it was enough to ruffle his opponent, plant a seed of doubt in that cybernetic brain of his, and with just metres to go, he hoped he could stay in front for long enough – if he could only reach the finish line in time…

Ever since he was small, Raffi Delgado had been frustrated by time. It seemed to him the arch-deceiver – promising so much at the dawn of each new day, and then, before he knew it, slipping away from him like sand through his fingers – inevitable, inexorable, irretrievable. During the dull periods – studying fractal geometry or travelling on the Moon Shuttle to see his aunt – time moved with the speed of a growing toenail. But the joyful moments – the moments he lived for – seemed to end almost before they had properly begun.

For a Megacity boy of the late 22nd century, even one from the lowly outlands, there was no shortage of entertainment on offer, but Raffi's parents, determined he do well at school, strictly rationed his leisure time: just one hour each weekday evening, and six hours on weekends. Within those rigidly enforced parcels of time, Raffi was free to pursue his hobbies: wave-riding on Londaris Channel, catching a motion media show on sensovision, or – his favourite – hoverbike racing. But, of course, these activities always ended much too quickly. He grew to hate the chime of the clock, the dimming of the daylight, the messages from his mother – time's merciless sentinels reminding him that the fun would soon be over.

But now, as the finish line approached, time did a strange thing. It seemed to slow, expand, elongate. Or was it just that Raffi's senses had become super-refined, so that the infinitesimally brief events within each second became apparent to him? He saw the slow flapping of Red's collar like the wingbeat of an approaching vulture, the twitching of the boy's jaw muscles, the steady progress of his bike's prow as – millimetre by millimetre – it gained on Raffi's. But in his hyper-aware state, Raffi knew long before Red that he wasn't going to be caught. Time had run out on Red Oakes. Clear centimetres remained between them as Raffi's prow breasted the light-sword and he was bathed in the silver glow of victory.

Later, as he stood there on the podium, holding his championship trophy in one hand and his retrieved St Christopher in the other, Raffi's joy was diluted by a small pang of regret. Time, he acknowledged, was the real victor today. In crossing the finish line, he had also reached the end of childhood's road. Tomorrow, he would turn 18, and after that even rationed pleasures would end. He looked into the chastened eyes of Red, standing a step lower, half-heartedly displaying his medal for second place, and felt an unexpected stab of envy. Red was 12 months younger than Raffi, and could compete again next year.

CHAPTER TWO

⧗

BUYING TIME

When the birthday celebrations were over and his friends had gone home, Raffi was ushered into his father's study. 'The good news,' said his dad, 'is that your uncle's bequest has come through. The money is in your account. Spend it wisely, my son. It should be enough to take you through the next couple of years until you start earning.' Then Felipe Delgado's face turned more serious. 'Son, you're 18 now and you have to start taking life more seriously. You must forget the hoverbike racing and start thinking about your Vocational Training.'

Raffi had expected to hear these words, but still they saddened him deeply – especially the last two. His mother had sometimes mentioned how she used to be a dancer. 'Why don't you dance any more, mum?' he once asked her. 'I had to do my Vocational Training,' she had replied. 'Then I worked for Universal Systems, then I met your father, then I had you. What time did I have for dancing?' To Raffi, Vocational Training was the first step on the conveyor belt to

Responsible Middle Age. He wanted no part of it. And yet what choice did he have? Cruel time was on the march. Tomorrow he would have to take his place, along with everyone else who had been born 18 years ago, at the local Vocational Training Centre. They would study his school test results and subject him to a series of personality tests. Then a computer would issue him with his Specialisation. From that point on, Raffi's life would be as well-plotted as a route on a map.

After his talk with his father, Raffi retired to his bedroom feeling miserable. He looked out of his south-facing window at the grey-pink Megacity sunset. The skyline was dominated by tall, slender towers and mushroom-shaped edifices. Each one sparkled with the lights of countless office windows: a metropolis of 30 million souls and all of them slaving away. For what?! So they could afford to rent a domicile and raise children – children who would grow up into a new generation of work-slaves!

In the distance he saw the bright oval disk of the Paridex Municipal Hover Track – scene of yesterday's triumph – the last race he would ever take part in. The misery of this thought was about to overwhelm him when, just above the stadium, his eye was caught by a sky-vert. It winked at him from the side of a fluffy pink cloud. YOU HAVE ALL THE TIME IN THE WORLD it read in big letters. Beneath that was an hourglass shape and the words: Buy yourself a little extra at the Time Store.

The Time Store?

Raffi stared at the cloud for some minutes in silence. Then he spoke to his MAID: 'Jane?'

A circular light pulsed on his bedroom wall. 'Yes Raffi. How can I help you?' came a calm female voice.

'What is the Time Store?'

'The Time Store is a new organisation,' replied Jane. 'It is operating behind heavy cybershields, so I cannot access many details. According to its own publicity release, the Time Store functions just like a traditional retail outlet – except that instead of selling goods, it sells time.'

'How does that work then?'

'Again I do not have many details.' Jane paused for a moment as she trawled the web for any relevant information. 'The store sells blocks of time in a range of sizes – anything from a day to a year,' she said.

'It can sell you a year?' queried Raffi, trying to remain calm.

'That is correct.'

Raffi was astounded. This was like the answer to a prayer. He could go to the Time Store tomorrow at 9 a.m., buy a year, and still be in time for his enrollment at the VTC at 10. His parents would never need to know!

'How do I go about buying a year?'

'I believe you simply go to the store and pay them. There is also a purchase form that you will need to complete. I can fill in the form for you if you like.'

'Yes, please do that, Jane.'

An image of a form filled his wall screen. In the top corner was the same black hourglass symbol Raffi had seen on the sky-vert. Raffi's details rapidly appeared in the spaces on the form.

'It requires a medical report,' said Jane. 'Do I have permission to include your latest one?'

'Yes, go ahead.'

'I have to read the following statement to you,' said Jane. She began reciting a long, dull statement full of legal language about terms and conditions.

Raffi interrupted. 'Jane, pretend you've read it to me, okay? Just tell me if there's anything in there that I ought to know about.'

'The only issue I can see is your age. Anyone under 21 requires the signature of a parent or guardian.'

This could be a problem. Raffi thought for a moment....

He could forge his mother's biometric signature. He had done this once before when his mum refused to give him permission to enter a hover-bike competition. He should still have the holoscan files he'd made that time. His mother was a heavy sleeper. It had been easy enough to make holoscans of her fingerprints and eyes while she slept.

'Jane, can you retrieve my mum's bio-sig for me? It's a file I made about a month ago.'

Almost instantly, holoscans of his mother's eyes and hands appeared in the middle of the room. They were a little flickery – he'd done them in a hurry.

When MAIDs (Multitasking Autonomous Interactive Devices) first came on the scene a few decades earlier, people were concerned that they might be used by governments or corporations as a way of spying on the public. To answer these fears, MAIDs were programmed with obedient and unquestioning personalities. This is why Jane did not ask Raffi why he kept a copy of his mother's bio-sig on his hard drive, nor query his request to upload it to the Time Store form.

Once Raffi had supplied his own biometric signature, the task was done. Jane transferred the form and its attachments to Raffi's handcom, ready for him to take to the Time Store in the morning.

'You're off early,' said Maria Delgado to her son the following morning. 'You don't have to be at the VTC till 10.'

Raffi wiped the crumbs of toast from his mouth and kissed his mum on the cheek. 'I'm just keen to get started on my new life,' he told her. 'I can't wait to find out what my Specialisation is.'

'I'm proud of you, Raffi,' said Maria. The front door of their domicile slid shut. For a moment Raffi stood there, making a mental photo of his mother's smiling face. Then he turned and ran towards the bank of levitators on the far side of the plaza. Adrenaline coursed through him. He felt like singing at the top of his voice. He joined a group of unsmiling commuters on the glowing disk of a levitator. Raffi hummed a loud and raucous tune as it whisked them down, by means of magnetic levitation, through a transparent tube to street level. Some of the commuters eyed him nervously, then exchanged discreet glances. Raffi caught a hoverbus to Channel Island City, urging it faster and cursing the commuters who auto-flagged it at every block. He wanted to be there the moment the doors opened. They reached the Northern Causeway at Dover at 8.35, and glided onto the artificial island in the centre of the Channel 10 minutes later. The bus stopped outside the office of the Time Store in Blue Yonder Street at 8.57. The building was tall and perfectly black. No windows were visible. Raffi joined the back of a long queue that had already formed in front of its tall black doors.

At 9.00, a large hologram flicked on above their heads. The hologram was a giant, rotating hourglass symbol. The doors swung open to reveal a brightly lit and shiny-floored interior. The crowd, including Raffi, surged through the narrow doorway into the foyer. In the centre of the vast hall was a round black pillar of enormous diameter. Set within the pillar were a series of small, glass-fronted offices. Raffi could see four of these from where he stood. He assumed there must be another four on the far side of the pillar. Officials strode forward wearing grey uniforms. On the left side of each of their chests was the same hourglass insignia, slowly rotating through the weave of the uniforms' electronic fabric. They directed each customer to one of glass-fronted booths. Raffi joined the queue for Booth Six. He looked at his watch: 9.15. His year had better not take too long or he would be late for the VTC!

At 9.24, he reached the head of the queue. Two minutes later a green light flashed and the booth's door slid open. As Raffi entered the booth, a tall, balding man sprang up from behind a small desk. His thin lips expanded into a smile and he extended a long, bony arm. 'I'm Luther Prefix,' he said. 'Welcome to the Time Store... Is your Purchase Form on there?' He pointed a finger at the handcom in Raffi's belt.

Raffi nodded.

'Well then would you be so kind...?' He gestured to the lapcom on his desk. Raffi transferred the form.

Prefix crouched over the desk and studied the screen, emitting little nods and clicks of approval. His shiny, moon-coloured pate bobbed up and down. 'So you want to buy a year?'

'That's right.'

'You're aware of the physics involved, I take it?'

'How do you mean?'

Prefix glared at him. 'The transactions of this institution are bound by a number of regulations, procedures and operational standards, generally known as the laws of the universe. Basic Newtonian principles, plus a few more recently discovered ones. It's in the fineprint on the form.'

Raffi felt as though he was being treated like a child. 'Look, I just want to buy some time. I'm not interested in a science lecture.'

'Understood,' smiled Prefix. 'Tell me, how are you planning to spend your year? If you want to work, we have some interesting employment opportunities. If you're planning to study, we can offer some fascinating courses.'

'I don't want to work or study,' said Raffi. 'Those are exactly the things I'm trying to escape from.'

'Aha, aren't we all?' Prefix chortled. 'That word, escape, must have crossed the lips of almost every person I see coming through this office. Escape from school, escape from Vocational Training, escape from work. Yes, the Time Store does offer the ultimate escape, and, of course, we can promise to have you back long before anyone's noticed you're gone… So then it's not work or study you want? In that case, we can offer you a range of leisure options, from watersports to air tennis, and from virtu-real gaming to the latest motion media releases.'

'How much will all this cost, Mr Prefix?'

The man's long fingers went to work on the lapcom's keyboard. 'You'll be pleased to hear we're offering a 10 percent discount as it's our first month of trading.' He stopped pressing buttons and squinted at the screen. 'The total sum you will need to pay – and this includes luxury accommodation with MAID service – i-i-is… 20,000 u-dolls… Of course you will also need funds to cover your living expenses for the next twelve months.'

Raffi had inherited 45,000 u-dolls from his Uncle Elias – easily enough to buy a year and spend it in comfort. It would leave nothing for his life during the two years of Vocational Training, but he wasn't going to worry about that now.

'So when can I start?' he asked.

'As soon as the funds have cleared your account. If you're happy with everything, I can activate payment now.'

Raffi took a deep breath. 'Go ahead.'

CHAPTER THREE

⌛

WELCOME TO THE CHRONOSPHERE

'ongratulations,' said Luther Prefix once Raffi's payment had gone through. The man seized Raffi's hand in a cool, bony grip. 'You're now free to enter the Hyperbaric Chronosphere.'

'The what?' Raffi's smile faded.

'The Hyperbaric Chronosphere, or Chronosphere for short.'

'What's that?'

'Well to put it very simply, it's like a bubble of compressed time. In the Chronosphere, time moves around half a million times slower than it does in the real world, so that a whole year can be experienced in one Earth minute.'

Raffi gulped. 'How, how exactly does that work then?'

'I thought you didn't want a science lecture.'

'No, I don't, but I just want to… have some idea of, of what I'm letting myself in for.'

Luther laughed, sounding like a park crow lording it over the pigeons. 'You're not the first to express anxiety at this stage of the process, Mr Delgado. People love the idea of buying time in theory, but when it comes to the practicalities, it all gets a little startling. How, after all, can this mysterious element that we travel through, which we call time, be trapped in a bubble and slowed down or speeded up at will? It doesn't make sense, does it? When we consider time, we tend to think of clocks steadily ticking their way through the seconds, minutes and hours at a pace that never varies. Each second, minute and hour is precisely the same length as the one that went before and the one that will follow, and so on forever. But that vision of time is manmade. It is a convenient illusion that helps us all to live and work and catch trains and meet girlfriends and so on.

'In truth, time is nothing more than a state of mind. For every one of us it moves at a different speed, a speed that fluctuates with each passing mood. When you're having fun it goes a lot faster than when you're bored, for example. For a child a summer can seem like forever, while for an adult, the years can flash by in no time at all. Now, what if we were able to manipulate those mind-driven fluctuations? Rather than be governed by time, we would be able to experience its passage at whatever velocity we choose…

'And that is exactly what the clever boffins at the Time Store Research Facility have managed to do. They've figured out the mental processes that govern our experience of time. They've studied the brainwaves of boredom, and found the frequency of fun. Then they learned how to control them. The Chronosphere exploits our natural ability to stretch or speed up time and takes it further – much, much further. And that, in highly simplified terms, is how it works.'

'But…?' Raffi knew he had more questions, but was unsure how to express them. The whole idea sounded too ludicrous. Were they stretching time itself here or just his experience of time? And did it even matter? All that mattered, surely, was that he was going to add a whole extra year to his life. That was 52 weeks, nearly 9,000 extra hours, over half a million extra minutes. This was payback time for all those happy moments that had been stolen from him since he was too young to remember.

Prefix raised his eyebrows. 'But?'

'But nothing,' said Raffi. 'I'm ready now. Let's do it. In fact, let's do it right now.'

'Don't you want to go home? Pack a few things? A year is a long time. You may want to take something familiar with you – a photo of your mother perhaps?'

Raffi thought for a moment before shaking his head. 'There's nothing I want from home' he said. 'I'll buy anything I need. There are stores in there, right?'

'Oh yes: stores, eathouses, bars, almost everything you could ever want or need.'

Prefix gave him a plastic card. 'Hand this in at the reception desk when you arrive. It has all your details on it.' He pressed a button on his desk and the wall behind him slid open. An orange glow filled the room. Raffi gasped.

Behind Luther Prefix lay a long tunnel. Its smooth, curving, white sides were interrupted every few metres by strips of pulsating orange light. To Raffi's perspective they appeared like concentric orange rings, surrounding the small metal door that lay at the far end of the tunnel.

'This way, Mr Delgado' ushered Prefix.

Raffi hesitated.

'You have nothing to fear,' Prefix reassured him. 'This is Temp-Al Chamber Six.'

'Temple…?'

'Temp-al is short for temporal alignment. It's one of eight entry points to the Chronosphere. Slowing your internal time-speed to half a million seconds per second is quite something for your body and mind to go through all at once. The temp-al chamber allows for a more gradual deceleration. It's quite comfortable, I assure you.'

Gingerly, Raffi stepped onto the tunnel floor. He felt Luther's hand on his arm. 'This is where I bid you farewell, Mr Delgado. Enjoy your stay in the Chronosphere. I'll see you back here in a year, your time.'

Raffi began to walk forward. As he passed through the first orange strip, a strange shimmery feeling passed through his body. It was not unpleasant and it stopped almost immediately. Yet it left him feeling slightly altered – he could not say how. He looked back. Luther Prefix was gone, replaced by a blank white wall. He continued walking, feeling the same odd shimmer and sense of having been subtly changed as he passed through each successive strip. As he progressed, he had the odd feeling that the distance between each orange strip was getting longer, although he was sure that on first viewing they had looked equidistant. Even increasing his pace, it still took him longer each time to reach the next strip. The further he went, the more exhausted he became. And was it his imagination, or was he actually walking uphill? After passing through seven strips, he stopped in surprise. There were just two more strips between him and the door, yet the door looked no nearer than when he had started. From Prefix's booth the tunnel had appeared no more than 50 metres long. He must have walked four times that distance at least.

Raffi felt himself begin to sweat. Something was wrong. What if he could never reach the door? What if there was no end to this tunnel and he was caught in some nightmarish optical illusion? Perhaps the whole thing was a trap! What a fool he'd been, handing over 20,000 u-dolls to an organisation he knew nothing about! How gullible to believe they could actually slow or speed up time – the very idea now seemed quite ridiculous. He broke into a run. The pain in his legs and chest was intense, but he refused to stop. When he reached the next orange strip, its shimmery touch felt like a wave crashing through his aching body. He allowed himself a short rest, hands on knees, panting like a marathon runner. Then he took off again. The gradient of the corridor seemed to increase as he went. After what felt like about 20 more minutes of jogging and walking, he passed through the final orange strip. He didn't even look up to see how far away the door was: he didn't want to risk the disappointment. If he just kept blindly running, he told himself, he must eventually get there. He launched himself on the final leg, running for as long as he could, then walking, then running again, keeping his eyes tightly closed all the while. The end came suddenly, when he least expected it: his head hit something hard and he keeled over.

Dazed, Raffi looked up. The door was there, as real and solid as any door. Above the door a light flashed red and a voice announced: 'Temporal alignment is now complete. Prepare to leave the temp-al chamber.' The light flashed green and the door slid open. Raffi stumbled into an enormous space with a shiny marble floor, dotted with pot plants and water features. At the far end – at the very, very faraway end – was a long desk. The roof soared high above him. It looked like a cross between the lobby of a posh hotel and a spaceship hangar. Breathless and sweaty, Raffi began crossing the expanse of marble floor. The sounds of trickling water and soft orchestral music calmed his heart. He felt somehow lighter since his experience in the Temp-Al Chamber, with more spring in his step. Despite his recent exertions, his muscles seemed to pulse with energy. He caught sight of his reflection in a mirror and was relieved to see a familiar-looking dark-haired boy glancing back at him. In less time than he would have thought possible, he reached the reception desk and joined a queue of five or six people. Behind the desk was a green-uniformed android with a smooth, shiny face and a pleasant perma-smile.

When it was Raffi's turn to be served, he handed the android the card Luther Prefix had given him. The android scanned the surface of the card. 'Raphael Delgado? Welcome to the Chronosphere. We hope your stay here will be a pleasant one. Please place your left index finger on the scanpad. Thankyou. Now say your name into this microphone.' Raffi did so. 'Excellent. Your print and voice are now recognized by Flora, your domicile MAID, and she will answer only to you. You will be occupying Domicile 3898 on Floor 38 of Time Tower. From there I believe you have an excellent view across Periodic Park towards Lake Perpetuity. I see you have no luggage, Mr Delgado, so I assume you won't be requiring the assistance of a porter-droid. To reach Time Tower, simply go to the set of doors on the left and wait. The next transradial should be here in a few minutes.'

Raffi walked – almost glided – over to the brushed metal doors. Before long they slid open to reveal the interior of a 'transradial': it was long, transparent and tube-shaped, apart from its flat black floor. Two rows of seating ran along its length from front to rear. Raffi took a seat close to the tube's bulbous front. The doors closed behind him and the transradial began to move smoothly forwards into the interior of the Chronosphere. A metallic voice announced: 'Next stop: Solstice Square.'

Looking around him, Raffi got his first sense of the scale of the place that was to be his home for the next year – and it made him gasp. The Chronosphere appeared to be a vast, sunlit, blue-skied dome, dwarfing even the giant lobby he had just departed. It was dominated by the sight straight ahead of him: an enormous hourglass-shaped structure that stood at least a kilometre high. The edifice had to be more than three kilometres away, though its size made it appear closer. Its inverted-dome-shaped top seemed to reach all the way to the highest point of the dome's sky-coloured roof. That, he assumed, was Time

Tower. Its thousands of windows glittered in the false sunlight of the Chronosphere, turning it, in Raffi's fanciful mind, into the sparkling silver dress of a giant, curvy woman. Viewing it in this way, her head would be above the dome and her feet below the ground. But her narrow waist and the great swell of her hips and bust were on gorgeous display from wherever you were within the dome. Fanning outwards from the hem of her skirt were streets lined with stores, eathouses and bars. When these ended, the roads continued on into a landscape of parkland, lakes, rivers, forests and low, rolling hills. The 'sky' of the dome was eggshell blue with a smattering of fluffy white 'clouds'. The light was just like summer sunlight without the sun – bright but not harsh on the eyes. The transradial glided to a stop, but Raffi scarcely noticed, still mesmerised by the view.

'You're new here, aren't you?' came a voice behind Raffi.

He turned to see a boy of about his own age, who had just boarded. The boy had very pale skin and hair as blond as Raffi's was dark.

'You can tell?' Raffi smiled back.

'Everyone stares like that when they first arrive. It takes your breath away, doesn't it?' He took a seat next to Raffi, as the transradial recommenced its journey.

'It's amazing,' said Raffi. 'It almost feels like we're outside. How come we can't see this dome from everywhere in Londaris?'

'I've often wondered about that myself. It doesn't make any sense. But then nor does the idea of compressed time, when you think about it. I'm Jonah, by the way. Jonah Grey.' The boy held up his hand, palm outwards, and Raffi clenched it. Jonah's hand was cool and slightly damp.

'Raffi Delgado. So how long are you here for?'

'A year. I've been here six months already.'

'Six months? But how? The Time Store only opened for business a few weeks ago.'

'You forget, six months is just half a minute out there! I probably only just beat you in here!'

'So it's true then! They really can slow down time?'

'Of course they can!' Jonah laughed, and his laugh became a series of coughs.

'You okay?'

Jonah held his hand up to indicate he was. Finally, he managed to say: 'Don't worry. Just the tail end of a cold. There are a few bugs flying around the Sphere, as you can imagine.'

Raffi blinked. For a second – perhaps less – he had glimpsed something quite horrifying. While Jonah had said '…as you can imagine', his face had suddenly changed into that of a very old man. The boy's fresh, pale skin had turned hideously wrinkled. His mouth had become a shrunken, toothless pit and his fair hair had turned to wild grey tufts that stuck out from the sides of his head.

Raffi clasped his mouth to prevent himself from crying out.

Jonah – now back to normal – looked at him. 'Are you okay?'

'I feel a bit nauseous,' gasped Raffi.

'That'll be time-sickness,' smiled Jonah. 'Takes a while to get used to travelling at this speed. It'll soon pass.'

'Solstice and Fourth,' came the announcement. Glass doors in the side of the transradial slid open. The green fields that had bordered the track since the lobby had been displaced by a more urban setting. Below the platform, Raffi glimpsed stores and bars bustling with people. He felt scared, but told himself it had just been his imagination playing tricks.

'Next stop: Time Tower.' Ten minutes later, the

transradial glided to a halt at the station beneath the giant hourglass. Raffi and Jonah stepped onto the platform and fought their way through the crowded platform towards the exit.

⧗

CHAPTER FOUR

Time Tower

affi followed Jonah onto a spiral glass conveyor that lifted them into the middle of a busy open concourse full of people and service-droids moving purposefully in every direction. 'This is the Lower Atrium of Time Tower,' Jonah explained. 'The central hub of the Chronosphere. From here you can go anywhere. Raffi followed Jonah's gaze upwards and got a shock. He saw now that Time Tower was not solid within, but hollow, and he was looking up into the great parabola of its lower half: up the giant lady's skirt, you might say! From the parabola's apex, which soared some 500 metres above their heads, transparent tubes radiated outwards, following the curve of the walls all the way to ground level, like the spokes of a dome-shaped umbrella. Through these tubes moved little glowing disks: levitators carrying people who, at this distance, resembled insects. Between the tubes were tier upon tier of internal balconies, some occupied by residents watching the world below. The air above the concourse was abuzz with hoverbike riders, flying between the domicile balconies or simply circling around in cruise mode.

Raffi felt almost drunk with the view, in the way he remembered feeling as a boy visiting the Basilica in New Rome.

'Listen,' said Jonah. 'A few of us are going out this evening. There's a music and light display at Periodic Park. You're very welcome to join us...'

'That's kind of you. Maybe I will.'

'Great. I'm in Domicile 10020 on the 100th floor. We're all meeting there at nineteen hundred hours. Just take the levitator or your hoverbike and we'll see you up there when you're ready.'

Raffi waved his new friend goodbye, and took a levitator to the 38th floor. The ascending platform of light slowed and stopped at his level. A door, slightly concave to match the gentle curvature of the giant dome, slid open. He walked through a narrow lobby. Muzak drizzled like fine, meaningless rain on his ears. At the end of the lobby, a corridor of doors curved out of view in either direction. After a short hike around the skirt of Lady Time at what he estimated to be around the height of her knee, he found Domicile 3898 and pressed his index finger to the scanpad. The door clicked softly open. The domicile was exactly as he expected: soft, shiny, self-cleaning bedding and upholstery; white, fluffy towels in the bathroom; MAID-controlled, voice-activated temperature and light settings: comfortable, functional and totally characterless. It was a base, nothing more. And it fulfilled that purpose perfectly.

He took a shower, while Flora, his personality-enhanced MAID, made a careful note of his preferred temperature and pressure settings 'so that he could always rely on the perfect shower in future'. Her voice had a soothingly older-sisterish quality – sweet, yet slightly stern. After his shower, he lay down in his white fluffy dressing gown, letting his mind go blank, while the bed slowly massaged his tired body.

Flora awoke him at 18.30. 'Time to get going Raffi. Do you want to try out some beauty accentuator facecream before you go and meet your friends? I've stocked some in your bathroom cabinet in case you do. I've also cleaned and ironed your clothes for you. Or perhaps you'd like to rent an outfit for the evening?'

Raffi blinked and sat up. He could always dial down her personality if he chose to, but he was actually amused by her sisterly concern. He hauled himself off the bed, took off his dressing gown and began to get dressed.

Still barefoot, and with shirt open to the waist, Raffi wandered onto the balcony to take in the view. The light had dimmed and the sky had changed to a deeper, velvety blue. The clouds were now lit from below with a fiery pink. It looked almost real. The air was regulated to the perfect early-evening setting of a light, warm breeze, and scented with something pleasant and summery – jasmine, perhaps? He caught snatches of soft jazz from a nearby domicile. Below him, lines of light radiated outward from the base of Time Tower. Along these thoroughfares, he saw crowds taking pre-dinner strolls or lounging at the many open-air bars. Between two of these boulevards of light Raffi noticed the dimmer, wedge-shaped outline of a large public garden. Silvery lamplight cast a mournful gleam on its lawns and pathways, occasionally picking out couples walking arm in arm or embracing on a bench by a fountain. In the distance beyond was the pale, satin-gold surface of Lake Perpetuity, dotted here and there with shadowy sails. Now and then a transradial, like a softly glowing neon tube, glided through the landscape, moving slowly between the outer edges of the dome and its hub.

Glancing aloft once more, Raffi's gaze was caught by the glorious swell of the upper part of Time Tower, which dominated a large portion of his sky. From this close it was hard to take it all in. Instead his eyes were drawn to the hundreds of individual domiciles, many of them now lit and clearly occupied by ant-sized residents. The way the tiers of lit balconies hung above him like a giant, gravity-defying chandelier was almost enough to induce vertigo. He wondered which little light up there was Domicile 10020. Buzzing below and all about this spectacle, like wasps around a nest, were perhaps a hundred hoverbikes. Telltale purple corona discharges glowed beneath them as their ionic propulsors jetted them this way and that with sudden bursts of speed. The riders he could see looked like kids, even younger than him.

Tethered to the docking point on the far side of the balcony was his own personal hoverbike. His heart gave a joyful leap just looking at it. Smaller and lighter than his beloved racing bike, it was nonetheless a stylish machine, with its black and silver trim, swept-back handlebars and undulating lines – unquestionably his mode of transport for the evening. He went back into his room and finished dressing. When he returned to the balcony, it was still only 18.45, but he couldn't be bothered to hang about any longer, waiting to be fashionably late. He climbed astride the bike.

'Have a lovely evening,' called Flora from behind him. 'And do be careful on that thing.'

Raffi put on his helmet, placed his index finger on the keypad and pressed the starter button, electrically charging the corona wire and ionising the compressed air in the intake chamber. The little machine shuddered. He released the airbrake with his right foot, then carefully rotated the right handlebar, opening the throttle. The hoverbike slid silently off the lip of the docking point into empty space. Raffi, who had never flown at this altitude before, gasped as he looked down and saw his foot framed by a plaza the size of a playing card. The bike felt small and lightweight between his legs, far too flimsy to support his weight. And yet somehow it hovered in perfect equilibrium, awaiting his next move. With his thumb he pushed the altimode, a small toggle on his left handlebar, away from him, and the craft rose upward through the darkening air. He began a slow, smooth ascent, following the curving contour of the tower, maintaining a distance of about twenty metres – close enough to see the domicile numbers emblazoned on the balconies, but not too close to appear intrusive. He counted off the floors: 60, 70, 80. By now he had reached the waist of Time Tower. Floor 100 was just a few stories below the narrowest point. He hovered there, then began to circle until he reached Domicile 10020. There was no one on the balcony, but the room beyond was lit. Raffi docked his machine, removed his helmet, and stepped onto the balcony.

He slid open the glass door leading to the bedroom. It was exactly the same layout as his. The only difference was that his room did not contain a beautiful girl sleeping on the bed.

CHAPTER FIVE

⧗

PERIODIC PARK

The girl awoke at the sound of Raffi's entrance. She sat up, her light blue eyes widening at the sight of him. Raffi had seen that look in a girl once before. That one had ended up kissing him. 'You must be Jonah's friend,' she said croakily. Her sleepy smile revealed a set of pearly-white teeth. Raffi searched in vain for evidence of cosmetic enhancement – surely such radiant golden skin, glossy blond hair, full red lips, cute nose and exotically sloping eyes couldn't occur naturally in a single face. She had to have a very good surgeon.

'Raffi Delgado,' said Raffi, offering his hand.

The girl hauled herself off the bed and stood up. She was tall – only a few centimetres shorter than Raffi. 'Lastara Blue,' she said. 'Pleased to meet you, Raffi.'

She gave his hand a brief squeeze. Raffi could see the faint flush in her cheeks, the tiny blond hairs on her bare arm. Clearly she was no hologram, nor gyndroid. 'Jonah's just getting dressed.'

'Are you… with Jonah?'

She shook her head and laughed. 'No, we're just friends. I'm with Dario.' Lucky Dario, thought Raffi.

'He's just picking up Sal,' she continued. 'They should be here any minute.' The girl reached into a handbag of the same pale metallic blue as her outfit and pulled out a discreet plastic pill dispenser. 'Want one?' she proffered. 'They're a kind of paradisiac. You'll enjoy the show so much more.'

'Why not? Thanks.'

Raffi took the pink pill and rolled it between his fingers thoughtfully. These days there were so many new drugs on the market, it was hard to keep up. 'What does this one do then?'

'Raises your sensitivity to music. Every note, every chord, sounds fresh. Believe me.' The pill melted instantly on his tongue and he felt the sweet residue trickle down his throat. Pills for love, pills for memory. Now a pill for music. Whatever next?

Jonah came in. He was dressed in dark colours that emphasised his blondness and pallor. 'Raffi. Good to see you. You've met Lastara.' He looked shorter than Raffi remembered; positively childlike next to the statuesque Miss Blue. 'Would you like a coolfizz before we head off?'

'That would be great,' said Raffi. 'I'm actually very thirsty.'

'That's due to your increased metabolic rate – something we all have to get used to in the Sphere,' explained Jonah. 'You'll find you have to eat and drink about twice as much as normal.'

'With no effect on your waistline, thank Bo,' added Lastara, with a smile.

Jonah disappeared into his tiny kitchen and came back with three cans. Raffi pressed lightly on the sides of the lid and it ejected itself into his hand with a small hiss. The drink was chilled and perfect, like pretty much everything so far.

He watched, amused, as Lastara fussed over Jonah's outfit, unfastening it at the top to reveal some of his pale, hairless chest. Jonah laughed and threatened to pour coolfizz over her.

The domicile door opened and in strode a large boy of muscular build. He had thin, half-smiling lips, a prominent, dimpled chin and deep brown eyes overhung with thick black brows. A handsome brute, and no mistake.

Lastara immediately terminated her game with Jonah and ran to the newcomer. 'Dario. I missed you, darling!'

'It's only been half an hour, sweetheart.'

'I know, but it felt like half a year!'

Raffi noticed Jonah's face on seeing the two lovebirds: the grimace, and the look in his eyes like flat champagne. He felt for the boy, but wondered also at his idiocy, falling for a girl like that.

So impressive was the sight of Dario that it took a little time for Raffi to notice his companion: the girl was small, slender and unremarkable in most respects, except perhaps for the blue colour of her cropped hair. While Lastara was all soft curves and golden skin, this one was hard-edged and pale, with a sharp nose and a cynical set to her thin lips. She stood by the door, saying nothing, meeting no one's eye. Raffi hardly had time to notice her before his hand was seized by Dario's great paw. 'Dario Brice,' he boomed. 'You must be Raffi. Very pleased to meet another new arrival. How much time did you buy?'

'A year.'

'A year! Blow me! I'd've bought a year if I could afford it.'

'We should get going,' said Jonah. 'Where's your bike, Dario?'

'At my dom. You wanna go pillion with me, sweetheart?'

'Uh-huh,' nodded Lastara. 'But what about Sal?'

The girl by the door shifted uncomfortably. 'I'll go by myself, it's fine,' she said in a low voice.

Jonah suddenly remembered himself. 'Sorry, you two haven't even been introduced. Sal Morrow, Raffi Delgado.'

Raffi briefly shook the girl's hand. She barely acknowledged him.

It was fully night in the 'Sphere' when the party departed. Far below, the neon strips of the radial boulevards shone brighter than ever. In the distance, Periodic Park was like a fantasy playground, with multicoloured lights suspended amid the trees and a laser light show slicing the air around a giant stage. 'That's where we're headed,' Jonah pointed.

Raffi closed his visor and his jacket against the chill. They flew low, almost skimming the tops of the trees. As they drew closer, Raffi saw that the stage was at one end of a huge oval depression in the ground with gently curving sides that served as a natural amphitheatre. Hundreds of people were already gathered on the grassy slopes. They set down in a relatively clear area to the right of the stage.

Soon the laser lights dimmed and a deep-register single glitterstring chord filled the air, like a momentous call to battle. Raffi felt the paradisiac kick in, boosting the richness and flavour of the sound quite deliciously. The chord was repeated, then overlaid with a series of high, rapid arpeggios that to Raffi sounded like notes falling from an angel's harp.

For the next couple of hours, Raffi was lost in the music and the light. Each note and chord progression, each bright, pulsating corridor and whirlpool in the sky, felt like a new discovery, a new territory. He realized that no matter how many pills he took, he would never experience it this way again, but that didn't bother him. The concert was the completion of a near-perfect day. And the best part was that scarcely one-twelfth of a second of real time had passed since he had crossed the threshold of the Sphere.

When it was over, the five of them sat or lay on the grass, saying little, their minds still buzzing with the experience. Their thoughts were suddenly interrupted by a chilling sound from somewhere to their right: it was like a boy's scream, and it stopped almost as soon as it started. 'Bobby?' came a girl's voice. 'Where are you Bobby?'

A torch flicked on. Raffi caught sight of the worried face of a young girl. Dario wandered over, followed by Jonah. 'Are you okay?' asked Dario.

'It's my boyfriend, Bobby. He was here just a second ago. Now he's gone. I don't know where he could have got to.'

'I wouldn't worry about it. He's probably seen a mate, or gone for an invitroburger. I'm sure he'll be back soon.'

'It's not like Bobby to just go off like that,' murmured the girl.

'What's his surname?' enquired Jonah.

'Laden, Domicile 1117.'

Jonah touched his collar stud, activating his wearable, and asked for Emergency Services. He gave them the details, and a few minutes later a couple of androids arrived on an airsearcher – like a large floating searchlight. The girl gave them a full description of the boy. They directed her to go and wait for them at the Missing Persons Office, then they departed.

The incident altered the mood of the group. They had all heard the cut-off scream just before the girlfriend raised the alarm. The boy had probably not just wandered off…

CHRONOSPHERE

At Jonah's suggestion, the group headed off to Transient Ridge on the far shore of Lake Perpetuity for something to eat. They touched down on a grassy bank filled with wooden tables and chairs. Loops of pastel-coloured gallium nitride lights lined a pathway along the lakeshore. Set back from here was a series of bars and eathouses, each of them with open frontages that displayed cosy, low-lit interiors.

Their eathouse of choice was a little place called Einstein's. Dario signalled to a passing server-droid and ordered Quantum Invitroburgers, Superstring Spaghetti and a jug of sweet, cola-flavoured coolfizz called Brownian Motion. Raffi was more ravenous than he could almost ever remember – an effect of the higher metabolic rate, no doubt.

'I hope that young lad turns up,' said Dario, as they tucked in.

'It's not the first disappearance,' commented Jonah. 'And it won't be the last.'

Raffi looked up. 'You mean others have disappeared?'

'No one's disappeared,' said Lastara.

'What about that 15-year-old girl last week on Calendar and Fifth?' pointed out Jonah. 'And three weeks ago, there was talk of a 17-year-old boy going missing in Tomorrow Fields.'

'Seems to be a pattern emerging,' said Raffi. 'They're all teenagers.'

'Of course they are,' laughed Lastara. 'And I bet you none of them actually disappeared. Like all young people – especially the types who come in here – they like to do their own thing. They've probably run off and joined one of the biker gangs that you see all the time around Spell Street and Solstice Park.'

'It could be the Moon Effect,' said Jonah.

'What's that?' asked Raffi.

'The Moon Effect is a complete myth,' scoffed Lastara.

'We don't know that for sure, sweetheart,' said Dario.

'What is the Moon Effect?' asked Raffi again.

Jonah tried to explain. 'Some people say that we cause a sort of imbalance just by being here. In the Chronosphere, we occupy time more densely than we occupy space, or maybe it's the other way round, I can never get my head around it. Anyway, it creates a sort of kink in space-time. The longer we spend in here, the worse this imbalance gets, and there is a theory, just a theory, that it can send us mad: the so-called Moon Effect.'

'So you think these disappearances have something to do with the Moon Effect?'

'It's just a thought,' said Jonah.

'What is it with you guys?' said Lastara. 'Life is obviously too perfect here, and perfection makes you uncomfortable. That must be why you keep trying to convince yourselves that things are going wrong. Honestly! Poor Raffi. He's only just arrived. What sort of place must he think he's come to?' She smiled at Raffi, as she had several times during the concert earlier.

'Or it could be Secrocon,' said Sal quietly. Everyone stopped talking. Sal rarely spoke, so it was always a significant moment when she did.

She turned to Raffi. 'Secrocon,' she explained for his benefit, 'is Chronosphere HQ. They run the show in here on behalf of the Time Store. It may be that they're the ones who are disappearing people.'

'Now I've heard everything,' moaned Lastara, putting down her fork. 'Why in hooly would Secrocon or the Time Store want to kidnap their own customers? Isn't it enough that they fleeced us for all they could get before they let us in?'

'I don't know,' said Sal. 'It's just a theory.'

Later, back at Time Tower, Raffi said goodnight to the others and returned to the balcony of Jonah's domicile. Before he could remount his hoverbike, he felt a gentle touch on his arm. He caught a scent of something sweet, yet slightly synthetic. He turned to see Lastara staring up at him. He was reminded of the look she gave him when they first saw each other. 'I just wanted to apologise for Jonah and Sal,' she said. 'I hope they didn't upset you with their crazy talk.'

'Don't worry about it,' said Raffi. He was unnerved by her expression and her closeness to him.

Her grip tightened on his arm and she pulled him towards her. Her lips felt soft against his. He didn't resist. For a long moment, he floated thoughtlessly in a world of sensations: warm, dreamy, subtle explorations that excited his heart and hinted at new and unexpected tomorrows. Then, through the blur of her fair hair, Raffi caught sight of a shadow moving behind the curtained door. Could it be Dario spying on them? But it wasn't only this that made him suddenly jump away from her. For just a second, even less, he was aware of a sickening change in Lastara's texture and appearance. The girl's mouth became dry as leather beneath his lips, and her face collapsed into a shrunken balloon of dense furrows and wrinkles, eyes clamped shut within cavernous sockets. Grey-blond hair clung like tenacious weeds to the fragile brown dome of her scalp. As with Jonah earlier, the repulsive vision was gone almost before he properly absorbed it. But he couldn't prevent the nausea it induced from leaking into his expression.

Lastara, now back to her radiant young self, looked hurt. 'Didn't you like that?' she asked.

'I'm sorry,' Raffi muttered. 'I liked it a lot. Honest. Just suffering a touch of time-sickness.'

'You're funny,' she giggled, stroking his face. 'Well, I suppose I mustn't keep you.' She stepped back from him. 'Goodnight, handsome.'

He gave her a quick, nervous smile, then turned and climbed astride his bike. As he began the descent towards his domicile, Raffi had to blink to erase the horrid memory of what he had just seen.

CHAPTER SIX

⧗

LAKE PERPETUITY

The following morning, Raffi awoke to the sound of birdsong and the smell of frying invitro-bacon. 'Good morning,' Flora sang gently. 'Breakfast is almost ready. Would you like an e-paper?'

'Mmhmm,' murmured Raffi. The paper that Flora sent floating down onto his bed was called Tower Times. The main news story was the light and music concert the night before. Raffi flipped through the journal by pressing a button at the bottom of the page. There was no mention of the disappearance after the show. In fact, it was all upbeat news about forthcoming events and trivial gossip about visiting celebrities. He scrunched up the digital paper and tossed it away.

'Flora, does anything bad ever happen in here?'

'No Raffi, I can't recall anything negative occurring in the 37 C-years that I have been functioning.'

Raffi grunted, then asked Flora to turn on the sensovision. Sensovision was television liberated from the box, with the images floating in three semi-transparent dimensions before the viewer's eyes, so that Raffi could watch it as he moved around the domicile. A cartoon soap was showing. 'Can I see the news channel?'

'We don't have a news channel, Raffi.'

'Because there is no news, right? – in a place where nothing ever happens.'

'Plenty happens in the Chronosphere,' Flora corrected him. 'Just not the sorts of things that make news.'

One chronospheric hour later, Raffi was floating down towards a golden shoreline, lapped by sparkling blue, frothy waves. The previous evening, he had arranged to meet the others here at Lake Perpetuity. He saw Sal seated on a towel, pale and withdrawn, blue hair covering her face, engrossed in an e-book. Near her, but closer to the waterline, lay the divine Miss Blue. Her tanned body enclosed in a silver bikini, she was a vision of youthful female beauty, making it all the harder to make sense of what he thought he'd seen the night before. Next to Lastara was the Adonis-like Dario Brice, wearing a pair of knee-length red shorts. He was sitting up and talking to Jonah, frail and slender-limbed, to his left. Dario, a model of charm and easy-going self-assurance, laughed at something Jonah said, then looked up as Raffi landed in a small puff of sand. The big guy leapt to his feet with the grace of a dancer. 'Raffi! Good to see you, mate! Glad you could make it! How the hell are you?' He clapped him on the back.

'Fine thanks, Dario. Anyone been in for a swim yet?'

Raffi glanced down at Lastara and caught her eye, but the girl didn't blush or betray any sign of their previous intimacy – just gave him a bland, welcoming smile.

'I was just about to go in,' said Dario. 'Coming sweetheart?'

'You guys swim if you want to,' murmured Lastara. 'I'm not moving.'

'What about you, Sal?'

'OK.' She put down her book, and stood up, dusting sand from her pale, skinny legs.

Dario, carrying his white waveboard under his arm, began wading in. The artificial sunlight gleamed like splashes of gold paint on his torso with its great ridges, bulges and valleys of muscle.

He gasped slightly as a cold wave slapped his stomach. When he was waist deep, he pushed himself onto the board and began to paddle away from shore with big, easy strokes of his brawny arms. Some thirty metres out, he hoisted himself smoothly up onto the board, spreading his legs and arms for balance. Then, crouching, he touched the board's surface and it instantly rose some 20 centimetres into the air. A wall of water vapour formed a hydrostatic barrier, retaining the cushion of compressed air beneath the board. Dario touched the board again, and it shot off at high speed across the lake, bouncing and plunging in great fountains of spray as it hit each wave. Dario wobbled a few times, but skillfully managed to keep his balance.

'He was waveriding champion at his school for three years in a row,' commented Lastara proudly. She was now propped on her elbows, watching her boyfriend's progress while shielding her eyes from the sunlight.

Sal tripped lightly through the surf before taking a dive into the waves. She began swimming a slow, precise breaststroke, close to shore.

'You going in, Raf?' asked Jonah. Perhaps he was angling to be alone with Lastara, but Raffi wasn't going to oblige. Not yet, anyway.

'Nah! Think I'll soak up some rays first.' He whipped off his singlet, aware of how poorly his physique compared to Dario's – although next to Jonah, he felt like Hercules.

Raffi lay back on his towel and shut his eyes. He heard a faint conversation between Jonah and Lastara as Jonah rubbed suncream into her shoulders. 'I'd stay here all my life, if I could,' Lastara was saying. 'Imagine, I could stay here for another sixty years, and it would only be an hour later out there.'

'You'd need a lot of dosh to stay in that long. And then there's the Moon Effect. We've no idea what that would do to you.'

'Oh, that's just a scary rumour. I keep telling you – there is no Moon Effect.'

'Well,' whispered Jonah. 'So long as you're here, I'd be happy to keep you company – if you don't mind me hanging around.'

'You're so sweet,' giggled Lastara. 'Hey, baby, that's enough on my shoulders. Can you do my back?'

They were quiet for a while, and Raffi heard Lastara's breathing slow. Jonah ceased his massage. 'She sleeps,' he sighed.

Raffi twisted around to look at him.

'Isn't she just beautiful,' whispered Jonah.

Raffi had to agree. 'She's also Dario's girlfriend,' he pointed out.

'That didn't stop you though, did it? Last night?' murmured Jonah, his eyes still fixed on her.

'You were the one watching us from behind the curtain then?'

Jonah looked at him miserably and nodded.

Raffi checked that Lastara was asleep. 'You won't tell Dario, will you?'

'No, of course not. I'm just jealous as hooly, that's all.

You've no idea what I'd give to kiss her the way you did.' He paused, doodling with his finger in the sand. 'I always knew I couldn't compete with Dario. I could live with that. I didn't mind getting the scraps – you know, the smiles, the flirtation, the back rubs. A girl like Lastara craves attention. And when Dario isn't around, I'll happily fill in. I could live the rest of my life like that, feeding off the leftovers – when each leftover tastes like a gourmet banquet, who wouldn't? But now, here you come, Raffi… I don't blame you. I'd do the same. But I can see it already – those looks she was giving you last night. I'm yesterday's news. You're the new "other man" in her life. And you're more than I ever was. She never walked up to me and kissed me goodnight like that.'

'Hey, Jonah,' said Raffi gently. 'I'm not planning on being anyone's "other man". And I don't want to go treading on anyone's toes.' He looked down at the golden girl to his right. Actually, his vow to Jonah was an easy one to make. For however beautiful she looked now, he simply couldn't shake off that horrific flash he'd caught of her as a wizened old corpse. So long as that sight continued to haunt him, there was no way he could start something with her, even if she'd been unattached and unpursued by anyone else.

Jonah's smile of relief was quickly replaced by a frown. He clutched his forehead.

'You okay?'

'Yeah. Just a headache. Don't worry. I get these all the time.'

The boy rummaged in his rucksack, and pulled out a bottle of pills. He swallowed a couple.

'Is this anything to do with that coughing fit you had yesterday?'

Jonah sat quietly a moment, nursing his head. 'Yeah, it's all connected. I suppose you're part of the gang now, so I may as well tell you. I've got something called Prolepsian Disease.

It's a very aggressive kind, and I haven't got long to live. Maybe a year, two years at most. My parents suggested I come in here to prolong my life while I'm still feeling relatively okay.'

Raffi's mouth felt dry. He struggled to think of something to say. 'Don't you think you should spend your remaining time with your family?'

'I prefer to be here. I hate the thought of seeing my parents try to be strong as they watch me get weaker.'

Understanding dawned on Raffi. 'You're not actually planning on leaving, are you?'

Jonah shook his head. 'I think it's better to see it through in the Sphere. There are brilliant doctors at the Med Centre. When I die, my family will get the news. It'll be hard for them, but far easier to deal with than watching me fade away.'

Raffi trembled inside. He looked at Jonah, feeling stupid and small in his presence. The boy was a giant, a hero. He remembered his laughter after the concert the night before. How could someone with a death sentence find anything to laugh at? He understood now why Jonah was prepared to feed off scraps from the table of Lastara Blue. What use was pride when you didn't have time? What use was anything when you didn't have time? When you lived so close to death, all that mattered in the end was love. Love and friendship.

A sudden drone like a swarm of hornets grew out of the west. They looked up to see a formation of hoverbikes appear low over the grey horizon, heading towards them.

Sal emerged from the waves, dripping, and covered herself with her towel. Dario followed her out and hung his towel around his shoulders, preferring to let the warm breeze dry him. He smacked Lastara on her rump, waking her up.

'Hey gorgeous. Who've you been dreaming about?'

'You, sweetheart,' she croaked. 'You know I always dream about you.'

'I wish I could believe you,' laughed Dario.

Sal was shivering, looking at the sky in a puzzled way. Raffi followed her gaze, then saw what was bothering her. Beneath one of the bikes that had just flown in, the purple plasma was fading and smoke was pouring out of the fuel cell. The bike was wheeling around chaotically and the rider was not in control. And then, quite suddenly, it dropped like a stone, heading straight for Dario…

CHAPTER SEVEN

⌛

Atomic Sands

Raffi saw the bike fall. He saw it was going to hit Dario. He knew he wouldn't reach him in time, nor even shout a warning. While his mind understood all this in an instant, his body, even his vocal cords, seemed stuck in glue. He heard a scream – Sal – and saw Dario, still laughing, start turning towards her. Then a shadow fell over him and a hot, smoking metal hulk rushed into view. Raffi closed his eyes. He waited for the crash, the screaming, but heard…

…nothing…

He opened his eyes, and what he saw made no sense. The bike, with its petrified rider, was there – but not smashed on the beach as it should have been, as the laws of gravity demanded. Instead, the bike was some three metres above the beach, directly above Dario, who by now had fallen back in shock and was staring, as they all were, at this apparition above his head. The bike and rider were frozen. The smoke that had been pouring from the bike's fuel cell was now still, like a cloud on a windless day. Then Raffi noticed the rider: a young lad in scarlet leathers looking like a screaming waxwork, head thrown back, every hair on his head flung upwards from his scalp as if fixed there by superstrong gel. With a shock of recognition, Raffi realised it was his old rival Red Oakes. What was he doing in here? And how could he have turned into a mid-air statue?

For several seconds no one moved or spoke. Then a deep growl came from just behind them. 'Don't move,' said the voice. 'Stay completely still.'

Raffi turned and saw a big man in a blue uniform with close-cropped grey hair standing on the summit of a dune. He was holding a smooth black gun. Its butt was jammed against his shoulder and he had his eye pinned to the sight. The gun's wide barrel extended about a quarter of a metre in front of him. The man was pointing the gun at Red. A cone-shaped portion of air extending from the gun's muzzle to the biker and his machine shimmered like a heat haze. Slowly the man descended from the dune onto the beach. The cone shortened as he approached.

When he reached them, he extended a narrow black rod from the base of the gun's grip. This turned out to be a tripod, which he planted firmly in the sand, ensuring that the muzzle and its cone of air continued to point at the biker. The man craned his neck towards the bike's underside, where fingers of frozen flame could be seen emerging from within the motionless smoke. 'Solid oxide fuel cell,' the man tutted. 'Looks like a seal fracture. Often happens at the high temperatures those things operate at, specially with all the punishment young lads like to mete out to their machines.' He turned to his gape-mouthed audience, and chuckled. 'I take it you folks have never witnessed a temporal decompression before.'

'Did that gun of yours make him stop like that?' asked Jonah, his voice shaking.

'You betcha.' He made a small adjustment to the gun's

setting. 'I'm Chrono-San Shep Tallis, by the way, of Secrocon Police. Pleased to meet you all.'

'What is that thing?' demanded Raffi.

'We call it an anabaric dilator. Creates a dilatory whirlpool – a little pocket of decompressed time – and our friend up there has been caught in that pocket. He's still falling – just half a million times slower than before.'

Jonah frowned. 'But I thought everyone in the Sphere experienced time at the same speed – that's how we all stay in sync.'

Tallis nodded. 'Normally, yes. But the dilators can override STV, at least for short periods.'

'STV?'

'That's Standard Temporal Velocity. It's a useful little tool for situations like this. But the override really eats up energy. The guys at HQ won't be best pleased if I keep the beam running too long, so I'm going to have to bring him back down now. 'Scuse me a tick.'

Shep returned to his dilator and adjusted a dial at the top of the barrel. The bike and its rider began to stir, then slowly sank to the beach, landing with the merest bounce. Red stared around him in disbelief, his movements extremely slow. 'Whhaaaatt … hhaaapp - pened?' he asked in a deep, rumbling voice that gradually rose to a more normal pitch as he regained temporal alignment. He blinked a few times, then pitched forwards onto the sand. The hoverbike, still belching smoke, fell the other way.

'Is he okay?' asked Sal.

'Oh, he'll be fine,' answered Tallis. 'I had to bring him up quite sharp because I saw what was happening only just in time. That can cause a temporary shock to the system, but it doesn't last long. Buy him an Alligator, that usually does the trick.'

'Alligator?' queried Jonah.

'Yeah, don't ask me why, but a glass of Alligator coolfizz is the best-known remedy for temporal whiplash. Works a treat. Now, folks, I must leave you to enjoy the rest of your day. Take care now.'

With that, Shep heaved his dilator onto his shoulder and walked back up the dune and out of sight.

'Thanks,' called Jonah. He looked at Dario. 'You should thank him. He saved your life.' But Dario, still in shock, could only shake his head.

Red's mates had fled, and his bike looked damaged beyond repair, so Jonah strapped the unconscious young man to the back of his own hoverbike, and soon the six of them were in the air heading for a small lakeside 'eat-and-meet' known as Atomic Sands.

Dario soon regained his spirits after downing a can or two of Alligator. 'Oh my dilator,' he sang, 'You time manipulator. You death frustrater. My love for you grows greater, with every glass of Alligator.'

As Shep Tallis had predicted, the drink also performed its magic on Red. 'Hello Master Oakes,' smiled Raffi once the boy had regained his senses.

'Raffi Delgado,' sneered the boy in his cut-glass Island City accent. 'How in hooly did you afford to get in here? Come into some money have we?'

'You know each other?' queried Jonah.

'Not socially, thank Bo,' sighed Red. 'We often race against each other at the Paridex Hover Track in North Londaris. I should have beaten you in that final, Delgado. I've no idea how you pipped me at the death like that. You'd been bleeding power since the end of the third lap. Are you sure you didn't cheat?'

Raffi could see the boy must have been torturing himself about the defeat over the last couple of days. No doubt Dookie Oakes, his dad, had been torturing him, too. With all the money he'd invested in Red, he probably thought the trophy should have been his by right.

'No, I didn't cheat.' Raffi withdrew the chunky metallic St Christopher from his pocket. 'Let's just say this brought me a bit of luck.'

'Luck,' Red almost howled. 'And when is it my turn for some luck?!'

'Your luck, my friend,' said Dario, 'arrived today instead.' He placed a hefty arm around the smaller lad's shoulders. 'Do you realize how close you came to dying just now? We're comrades, you and I, against the common enemy, the Grim Reaper, who very nearly just reaper-sessed our souls.' He raised his glass. 'So let's drink to life, to the air, and the fact that we're still breathing it.'

Raffi raised his glass along with the rest. He hadn't known Dario long, but he felt unexpectedly overjoyed, and quite choked up, at his lucky deliverance. Red, meanwhile, was soon flirting with Lastara, perhaps forgetting, or not quite appreciating, that he'd nearly killed her boyfriend. Red was not exactly a looker. His bionic enhancements had left him a bit boggle-eyed and heavy in the forehead. But despite this, and his short stature, he had a natural authority and an accent that oozed wealth and breeding. 'I recognise you from somewhere,' he schmoozed to Lastara. 'You must be an actress on one of the senso-soaps, or an e-mag model, for sure?' Lastara, quiet since the accident, was returning to form, as always enjoying the attentions of a male. Dario didn't seem to mind, or even notice, as he chatted happily to Jonah and Raffi.

'Coming so close to death,' he mused, 'gives you a whole new perspective…'

'I'm not sure you were ever that close to death,' said Sal. Raffi and Jonah turned to her, intrigued. Dario looked almost disappointed. 'Sorry Dario,' she said, without looking much like she meant it. 'But don't you think it odd that Chrono-San Tallis just happened to be in the right place at the right time, ready to fire his dilator-thing at Red?'

'Could have just been luck,' suggested Raffi.

She curled her lip disdainfully. 'Come on Raffi. It took a matter of seconds for Red's bike to fall out of the sky. Even if Tallis had been sitting on the beach right next to us, with his gun by his side, alert and ready to go, it would have been an amazing act of reflex to get the thing into position and firing before the bike hit the ground…'

'Go on then, Sal,' said Jonah. 'Give us your theory.'

'I reckon the whole Sphere is bristling with dilators. There are Shep Tallises behind every tree and bush, keeping an eye on us the whole time. That's why you never hear about any accidents. That's why there's no crime!'

Raffi nodded, recalling the lack of news in the e-paper that morning.

'I think they're using dilators all the time,' Sal continued '– not just on accident victims and criminals, but on all of us. After all, how would we know if we'd been dilated?'

'Why should they?' asked Raffi.

'It's a form of social control,' replied Sal. 'They use it to prevent us from seeing things they don't want us to see.'

'Such as?'

'I don't know,' she confessed. 'If I knew, I'd most likely be dead by now.'

CHAPTER EIGHT

⧗

INCIDENT ON
TOMORROW & THIRD

The weeks went by, and for Raffi it was like every summer holiday he'd ever dreamed of as a kid, but never quite had: days on the beach, hikes in the hills and forests, picnics by the river, or shopping jaunts in the boulevards. In the Chronosphere, there were always things to do and places to go. And the weather was always predictable: sun all day, with light rain every afternoon between 16.00 and 17.00, just to keep the landscape green and pleasant.

The only worrying aspect was the disappearances, which continued to occur on an almost weekly basis. The Tower Times was silent on the subject, remaining as blandly upbeat about life in the Sphere as ever, but Raffi and his friends heard about them through the reasonably efficient Time Tower grapevine. From the gossip they picked up, it seemed that these incidents always had two things in common: it was invariably teenagers who went missing and there were never any witnesses, despite the fact that they often vanished on crowded shopping streets in the middle of the day. Like the vast majority of teenagers in the Chronosphere, including Raffi's gang, the victims were here on their own or with friends – never with parents. In Lastara's view, the kids had joined biker gangs and were probably living rough somewhere in the hills or forests near the periphery. Sal for one found this story hard to believe: the Chronosphere was admittedly a big place, but she was certain that Secrocon had tabs on everyone, and 'disappearing' wasn't as easy as Lastara made out.

Raffi and his gang were not entirely inseparable. They also found time to pursue their own individual interests. Jonah spent most mornings at the Learning Centre on Solstice Square, taking classes in biosciences and engineering to make up for all the education he'd missed out on during his illness. Lastara did some e-mag modelling when she wasn't shopping or sunbathing. She also went to auditions, hoping to break into one of the many 'reality' soaps that were downloadable daily on sensovision. Dario paid for extensions to his time in the Sphere by working part-time in an eathouse on Transient Ridge. He also found several hours each day to play air tennis and enter wave-riding competitions. As for Sal, Raffi had no idea what she got up to in her own time. The name Marco was occasionally mentioned in proximity to hers, although Raffi was never clear who he was or what, if any, role he played in her life.

Raffi spent his time away from the gang racing at the Hover Track Arena on Solstice and Fourth. Here he couldn't avoid rubbing shoulders with Red Oakes. It turned out that the young cyborg had been despatched by his dad to the Chronosphere for some intensive retuning in time for another competition the following week. Dookie had studied recordings of the closing stages of the Paridex final and noted how his son had been visibly unsettled by Raffi's sudden spurt towards the end. He had decided that Red needed more focus and ruthlessness, and he paid his best neuroengineers to go into the Chronosphere with Red and, between them, come up with a new brain-computer interface to solve the problem.

'I just don't understand how they could have let the likes of you in here,' sneered Red whenever he saw Raffi at the track. 'Your dad's an assistant robot supervisor at Universal Systems for Bo-sakes. He must be on forty thou a year, tops. Did you rob someone? Are you a stowaway? You know I'll have to inform the authorities as soon as I find out.'

Raffi did his best to ignore him, but the insults couldn't fail to hurt and anger him – and it was never a good idea to feel hurt or angry while racing, when your nerves had to be ice-cool. Perhaps that was the reason for the accident he suffered on his third visit to the track. Taking a turn too sharply in an attempt to overtake another rider, his bike bounced and sparked off the side wall, causing him to somersault into the central gully. He wasn't badly hurt, but felt embarrassed at making such an elementary error, especially when Red started mocking him loudly in front of the other riders. 'You complete imbecile,' laughed Red. 'What the hooly did you think you were doing? Not even a total beginner would try a stunt like that.' He turned to the others in the arena and demanded, 'Who is this moron? Who even let him in here?'

Raffi knew the boy was still eaten up with bitterness at losing the Paridex final and that he had to suffer regular exposure to his dad's notorious temper. It couldn't be easy being Red Oakes, when half your humanity had been replaced by machine parts. Even so, Raffi couldn't help despising the boy and he dreaded crossing paths with him.

⧗

One morning, some three months into Raffi's stay, the friends
were hanging out at the arcade on Tomorrow and Third. In
theory they were there to help Lastara find an outfit to go
with a bag she had recently purchased, though in practice
they were all doing their own thing. While Lastara tried on
endless costumes in Superior Styles, her favourite boutique,
Sal was in a music store across the way, downloading tracks
to her wearable. Meanwhile, Jonah's attention had been
caught by the gaming room next door, and he was all masked
up in a total virtu-real bodysuit. His hand and body
movements implied he was flying a hypersonic aircraft
through a series of mountains or tall buildings. Dario, though
loyally accompanying Lastara in Superior Styles, was
actually lounging on a chair near the entrance, reading an e-
magazine and drinking from a can of coolfizz. Raffi lolled on
a bench near a fountain, taking in the scene through half-
closed eyes. He had almost nodded off when something
happened that thoroughly shook him from his torpor.

He became aware of a girl emerging out of the extreme left
of his field of vision – he noticed her because she was
strikingly pretty, with short, flame-red hair framing a pale,
heart-shaped face with green, wide-spaced eyes. The girl
walked slowly past Jonah and his wild gesticulations, past
Sal in the music store, then stopped outside Superior Styles,
looking at the window display. She turned her head and
waved back at someone – Raffi couldn't see who – gesturing
that she was going into the store. At that moment, Lastara
wasn't visible – she was probably in a changing room trying
something on. Dario looked up as the girl entered. Then,
putting down his coolfizz and magazine, he reached into his
rucksack and pulled out a large black gun-shaped object.
Raffi was surprised to note it looked just like Shep Tallis's
dilator. Dario stood up and aimed the muzzle of the gun at
the girl. She stopped dead in its shimmering cone. Dario then

swivelled a quarter circle to face the doorway, elongating the cone-shaped beam to form an arc that now included the store exterior. At this point, the scene abruptly changed: the red-haired girl had disappeared, and Dario was now back on his chair, reading his magazine. The dilator was nowhere in sight.

Raffi felt sick. He could scarcely believe what he had just witnessed.

A minute or so later, another girl entered the store. She was small, with a neat figure and brown and blond, spiky hair. She turned to Dario and asked him something. He shrugged and shook his head. Then she turned to someone else out of Raffi's sightline, perhaps a store-droid. The girl looked like she was struggling to remain calm. Raffi came closer so he could hear what was being said. She was now talking to the wearable in her collar, answering a series of questions, no doubt the standard questionnaire from Emergency Services. 'My name is Ry Bellonzi... Domicile 10838... the arcade on Tomorrow and Third... I'm her friend... Her name is Mira Chailin... She's 15.' Others were gathering now: store managers, members of the public, offering sympathy or simply soaking up the drama. Lastara reappeared from the rear of the store, sheathed in one of her hallmark metallic numbers: this one was pale green. She turned to Dario, puzzled at the crowd. He explained that a girl had disappeared.

In a state of semi-shock, Raffi went over to the gaming room. He shook Jonah. 'We've got to talk,' he said. 'I've seen something bad. Really bad.'

Jonah took off the mask. 'What is it?'

'There's been another disappearance. And I know who's responsible.'

'Go on then, who?'

Raffi flinched at the thought of what he had to reveal. 'It's

Dario. He did it with a dilator. I saw him pointing it at this girl, then at the arcade. He must have dilated all of us. The next second she was gone'

Even before he finished speaking he could see the disbelief in Jonah's face. 'Not Dario. No way, Raf. How can you say that? Dario would never do that.'

Raffi spelled it out again: 'I saw him, Jonah. He had the dilator.'

But Jonah still refused to believe him. 'So what are you saying? That he kidnapped her, or what?'

'I don't know what he did with her. All I know is that one minute she was there and the next minute she was gone.'

'What's going on?' It was Sal. Raffi told her what had happened.

'Dario? No! You've got it wrong, Raffi. Not Dario.'

Raffi stared at her, astonished. Sal, of all people – Sal, who was normally so ready to believe the worst of everything and everyone – should be prepared at least to acknowledge that he might be telling the truth. What was wrong with them? He shook his head and walked away. 'Ask him then,' he challenged Jonah and Sal. 'Ask him if he has a dilator. I dare you. Or perhaps you're both just scared of the truth.'

'Cool it, Raffi,' said Sal. 'You got it wrong. Can't you just accept that?'

A blue-flashing airsearcher began to circle like a flying saucer overhead. Raffi watched as Jonah and Sal went over to join Dario and Lastara outside the boutique. The friends talked normally – no one seemed to be challenging Dario, or even asking him questions. They had simply dismissed Raffi's allegation as they might a madman's ravings. He felt sidelined. These so-called friends had closed ranks, shut him out.

'Well you can get stuffed then, the lot of you,' he murmured, and trudged away from the scene.

⧗

Much later, he called Jonah. Jonah sounded concerned. 'Where've you been, Raf? Why did you just scoot off like that? We've been looking for you. Left umpteen messages with Flora and on your voicemail.'

'I've been out.'

'What, all day? Where did you go?'

'Anywhere. Nowhere.' Raffi had spent most of the day riding the transradials, thinking.

'What's wrong, Raf? Why don't you come over to my place? We can have a drink and a chat.'

'You've got to believe me, Jonah.'

'About what? Dario?'

'I saw what I saw.'

'You were half asleep, Raf. Sal said so... Look, I'm not saying you don't think you saw something. But you just got it a bit wrong, that's all. Dario hasn't got a dilator. And you weren't dilated. None of us were. Think about it logically for a second. He'd've had to dilate hundreds of people. It was a busy arcade. Yet no one saw or felt anything odd, only you.'

'But they wouldn't, would they? That's the whole point about temporal decompression. From everyone's perspective, time just continues as normal. If I hadn't been looking in that particular direction, I wouldn't have noticed anything either. Didn't Sal say they were probably dilating us all the time, stopping us from seeing what they don't want us to see? Maybe she's right after all.'

'Sal's just a conspiracy theory fruitcake. She's always coming out with stuff like that. But even she wouldn't go so far as to accuse a friend of kidnapping, or whatever it is you're saying Dario did.' Jonah started to cough. It lasted a long time. When it was over, he cleared his throat. 'Come over to my place, Raffi. Let's have a drink.'

'Don't patronise me.'

'Raffi –'

'I'm going to the police.'

'What?'

'You heard me.'

Raffi waited for Jonah to speak. 'Well, if you do that…'

'Yes?'

'…You'll be out, Raf… You won't see me again. Nor the others.'

Raffi swallowed. 'Jonah, look, just suppose I'm right. Let's just say Dario did dilate the girl and kidnap her or whatever. Would that make things any different?'

'You're not right.'

'But just suppose…'

'This is pointless, Raffi.'

'OK, what if I got evidence?'

'What kind of evidence?'

'I don't know, maybe Dario left some clues behind at the scene. Or maybe one of the store-droids recorded it. Look, it doesn't matter. All I want to know is: would it change your attitude?'

Jonah sighed. 'Maybe it would. But you're not right. So this is a pointless conversation.'

Raffi switched off the phone.

It was after 21.00 when he returned to Superior Styles. The arcade was still full of shoppers – a more relaxed, late-night crowd. Raffi walked into the store. He didn't know exactly what he should be looking for, just hoped he would know it when he found it. There was no sign that anything untoward had taken place. He looked at the chair where Dario had sat. Nothing. Of course, Dario would have had plenty of time to remove anything to link him with the crime. Raffi sat down in the chair, and surveyed the scene. He looked over towards the park bench where he himself had sat that morning. He mentally reenacted Dario's movements. He could have dilated everyone in the store and then, in just two quick steps, pointed the gun out into the arcade, and…

He frowned. Actually, now he looked at it more carefully, the boutique was in a recessed corner, set back from the rest of the arcade. Because of its position, its interior couldn't be observed from anywhere in the arcade except the bench where Raffi had been sitting. Dario had chosen his location well. He need only dilate the store-droid, the girl, Lastara and Raffi, then shut the door, put up the closed sign, and get on with his work. There had been no need to dilate everyone after all.

He approached a female store-droid behind the counter. 'Excuse me, were you on duty here this morning when that girl disappeared?'

'Yes, sir.' She had the blandly welcoming, pretty features of all her kind.

'Did you see or record what happened?'

Instead of answering, she glanced towards someone else to Raffi's left, perhaps the manager. Raffi turned and was surprised to encounter the chubby features of Chrono-San Shep Tallis, the Secrocon agent who had saved Dario's life that day by the lake.

Tallis's eyes narrowed, then suddenly widened with recognition. 'What do you know, weren't you one of the young folk on the beach that day a few months ago? Am I right?'

'Yes, chrono-san. The name's Raphael Delgado. Thanks again for saving our friend's life.'

'You're welcome, son. Now would you mind explaining why you're here trying to do my job?'

Raffi blushed. He started to explain, then stopped, recalling Jonah's words on the phone. 'If you do that… you'll be out, Raf. You won't see me again.' He ground his teeth, thinking furiously. Damn it! It's the truth. He was doing this for Dario as much as for himself. Not to mention all Dario's future victims… 'I saw something, chrono-san,' he stammered. 'I believe I know who was responsible for the crime that took place here this morning.'

Tallis took a long look at him. 'Okay then, Master Delgado – who was it?'

CHAPTER NINE

CONFESSION

The following morning, Flora informed Raffi that his friend Dario had been arrested and was being held in a Police Centre cell.

Raffi hadn't slept at all the previous night. His eyes ached, and his gut hurt from stress. 'Can I visit him?'

'I'm afraid it's not allowed, Raffi.'

He cursed under his breath. 'Can you call Jonah for me.'

'I'll try.' A minute later, Flora reported that Jonah didn't wish to speak to him.

'Try Sal.'

'OK.'

Soon Sal's tired voice emerged from a small speaker by his bed. 'What is it, Raffi?'

'I turned him in, Sal. I had to.'

'You didn't have to,' she said simply. 'You made a mistake. A horrid mistake. And now Dario is paying the price.'

'I saw what I saw, Sal.'

'You think you did.'

'Is there any way we can get to see him?'

'I have a friend who's going to try to get us in. I'll be going down there later with Jonah.'

'What about Lastara?'

'Haven't you heard?'

'What?'

'Lastara dumped him. Or he dumped her. I'm not sure which. Anyway, they're not together anymore.'

'Uh huh.' This news, which would have made headlines in their little world yesterday, was now just a filler story somewhere on the inside pages. 'Sal, can I come with you? I'd like to see Dario.'

'No, Raffi. We'd rather you didn't. I'm sorry.' The connection died. He asked Flora to call her again, but Pierre, Sal's MAID, informed them that Sal didn't wish to take any more calls from Raffi.

'I need to see him,' Raffi told Flora. 'I need to look him in the eyes and tell him what I saw him do. I need to hear how he tries to explain himself. You have to get me in there, Flora. Don't you have any digital mates down there in the cells. Can't you pull some strings, or whatever the computer equivalent of that is?'

'I'm sorry, Raffi. I understand how you feel, but I'm bound by the rules of the Time Store Corporation. There's nothing I can do.'

Then he had an idea. 'Get me Shep Tallis at the Police Centre, would you?'

Tallis was soon on the speaker, sounding busy. 'Yes, how can I help, young man? Hope this is urgent.'

'Chrono-San Tallis, has Dario confessed yet?'

'Confessed?' The police officer sounded surprised at the question. 'Er... yes. Yes, he confessed alright. We're grateful for your help, by the way. You've removed a menace from our streets. Now thankyou and good day.'

'But wait, chrono-san. That's not all.' This was not the

answer Raffi had been expecting. He had planned to offer his services to Tallis as an interrogator. He was sure Dario would find it harder to lie to him than to an anonymous policeman. But if Dario had confessed, that changed everything. Why were Sal and Jonah still shutting him out? 'What exactly did he confess to? What did he do with the girl?'

'That's not something I'm at liberty to divulge.'

'Can you at least tell me if the girl is safe?'

'Yes, I understand the girl is quite safe and well.'

'So what happens next? What will happen to Dario?'

'Oh, he'll serve a short sentence, and then be expelled I should imagine.'

'Sentence? I don't understand. He hasn't been tried yet, or found guilty.'

Tallis chuckled. 'That's pretty quaint, young man. What period of history do you think you're living in? We're a private police and criminal justice service representing the shareholders of Time Store Incorporated. Our obligations are to those good people, and to them alone. It's simply not cost effective to run the kind of full-scale judicial system you're talking about for the occasional petty criminal who wanders in here. Do you have any idea how much judges cost these days? Besides, the lad was a menace. He was using a dilator for nefarious purposes and with him off the streets, the Sphere is a little bit safer this morning. Now get out there and enjoy it. Have a good day.' The speaker fell silent.

Raffi was worried. What sort of system had he delivered Dario into? He had always heard there were strict safeguards in place to protect the rights of suspects, even in privately run criminal justice services. The policeman claimed that Dario had confessed, but who was to say he really had, or under what circumstances?

He hurriedly got dressed and rode his hoverbike to the 130th floor of Time Tower, where Lastara had her domicile.

He hoped she wouldn't reject him as the others had done. Perhaps he and she could figure out some way of getting in to see Dario. He docked on her balcony, then quietly knocked on the curtained glass door.

An unexpected and most unwelcome face peered out at him. To judge from Red Oakes' expression, the feeling was mutual.

'What the blazes are you doing here, Delgado?'

'I've come to see Lastara.'

'She's not seeing anyone right now – least of all you.'

'Then what are you doing here? I didn't know you were friends with her.'

'There's a lot you don't –'

'Who is it?' Lastara's voice seemed all clogged up with tears.

'Raffi,' he called, over Red's head. 'Can I come in?'

'Of course,' she said. Red reluctantly stood aside for him.

Lastara lay on the bed, used tissues scattered around her like little white roses. Her eyes were puffy and her hair a mess, but the effect was still impressive, almost artfully so.

'Look, I think I'll push off, old girl' said Red edgily, 'unless there's anything else you need.' Raffi guessed that the antipathy he inspired in Red was so intense, the young man could barely tolerate being in the same room as him without letting the insults fly – and since he didn't want to expose this ugly side of himself to Lastara, his only option was to flee.

'What was he doing here?' Raffi asked when the door had closed.

'Oh, Red's been a good friend,' was all she said. 'I suppose you heard about me and Dario?' Raffi was confused. Why was she talking about their relationship? Surely Dario being in custody was far more serious. 'I didn't want to break up with him,' she continued. 'But the situation was rather forced on me. Obviously I can't go out with a criminal. If I'm going to make it as a star of sensovision, I can't afford even a hint of scandal at this early stage of my career. You know what those celebrity newsdogs are like. They'll sniff out anything. I could have waited it out, I suppose, in the hope that he can clear his name. But that would be unfair on Dario. Better to make a clean break of it… Although of course, once he's out, who knows…' She gave a pale-lipped smile. 'I may wish to bask in his reflected notoriety.'

Raffi tried not to let his shock at this speech show. All he said was: 'I don't think he'll be allowed back into the Sphere after this. I heard they're going to eject him.'

She sighed. 'Oh well. That's it then. Still, it was fun while it lasted.'

'Do you want to see him? Talk to him about this?' asked Raffi. 'I'm going to try to get in to see him.'

'Oh no! I couldn't bear to. It would be too awful. Besides, he knows how I feel. I was with him when they came to arrest him. In the ten minutes we had before they took him away, I told him all I needed to. I told him I loved him but that I wouldn't wait for him like some dewy-eyed prison widow. He understands and accepts how important my career is to me.'

Raffi stood up. 'Well in that case, I'll have to go by myself.' The truth was he didn't wish to spend another minute in the girl's company. She was selfish to the core. For her, Dario had never been more than a handsome badge or trophy. She didn't actually care about him at all.

'Do you have to go right now?' implored Lastara. 'Why don't you stay a while? I have the perfect tonic for our unhappiness.' She opened a drawer and took out a plastic bottle containing green pills. 'Saporiacs!' she cried. 'They raise your sensitivity to all kinds of flavours. We could go out for a slap-up breakfast. That'll cheer us up!'

'No thanks, Lastara.'

Her face fell. 'I don't understand you, Raffi. I thought you were nice.'

'I thought the same about you once, Lastara,' said Raffi as he turned to go. 'Right now my thoughts are with Dario. As I assumed yours might be.'

Secrocon Police Centre was below the Time Tower atrium, one storey down from the Transradial Terminus. Raffi approached the central desk, where a grey-uniformed woman was standing.

'Can I help you, sir?'

Her skin looked too smooth and her dark red hair too glossy to be real. Her green eyes were unblinking and bright, like those of a doll.

'I would like to visit the prisoner, Dario Brice,' said Raffi.

'I'm sorry, that won't be possible.'

'Why not?'

'Company rules.'

'But I'm his best friend! I demand to see him!'

'I'm sorry, sir.'

Raffi thought for a moment. He couldn't just give up on Dario. There had to be something he could do. Then, suddenly, an idea hit him – clever, startling and utterly reckless.

'Actually, I've come to turn myself in,' he said.

'Turn yourself in?'

'Yes, I was an accomplice in the incident on Tomorrow and Third yesterday.'

'I see. Would you please follow me.'

The gyndroid moved from behind the desk, then walked swiftly across the grey-tiled lobby towards a blue door. Beneath the regulation grey jacket and trousers, Raffi caught a hint of female curves. He admired the engineering that had produced such a smooth, almost humanlike gait. The door melted into thin air at the touch of her finger on a scanpad, and she showed him into a square, featureless room containing just two chairs and a table. 'Please wait here, sir. The duty officer will be with you in a few minutes.'

The gyndroid left the room, and the blue door reappeared between them. Raffi rubbed his knuckle against the surface. It felt solid, like a dense plastic. There was no scanpad on this side of the door. Feeling rather like a prisoner already, Raffi sat on one of the chairs and waited. He didn't really have a plan. His only hope was that he would be taken down to the cells, and from there he might get to see Dario. A few minutes later, he heard footsteps outside. The door faded once again to reveal another grey uniform, this time worn by a big man with a large, hairy jaw and a thrusting, bearlike body.

'I'm Chrono-San Marvin Bullhammer,' he said striding in and sprawling himself in the other chair. 'I understand you're claiming involvement in yesterday's incident?' He rolled up his sleeves.

'That's right. I was on look-out for Dario Brice. My job was to make sure the coast was clear.'

'Hang on, hang on.' Bullhammer leaned forward and pressed a button set into a rectangular plate on the table. 'OK. What's your name?'

'Raphael Delgado.'

'Weren't you the kid who turned Brice in?'

'That's right.'

'So why didn't you turn yourself in then? Why wait till now?'

'My conscience got the better of me last night.'

Bullhammer grunted. 'Uh-huh. And why did you turn your mate in yesterday?'

'I – I didn't like the fact that he chose such a young girl.' Raffi hadn't expected such tough questioning. He hoped his nervousness wouldn't be misinterpreted.

'But that's what Brice does. That's his signature dish. He kidnapped a 16-year-old on Interim and Fourth last week. And a 15-year-old at that concert a few weeks ago.'

Raffi didn't know what to say. Could Dario have been responsible for the other disappearances as well? What had he done with all his victims? Where had he hidden them? He didn't seem like a kidnapper. But appearances could be… No. He wasn't going to go down that road – cast judgement on him as Secrocon had done before he'd been given a chance to defend himself. He had to see him first, look him in the eye. And to do that, he needed to keep his wits about him.

'Dario had promised to stop with the really young ones,' said Raffi carefully. 'He broke his word.'

Bullhammer stood. His dark brow furrowed. 'This sounds like baloney to me, Delgado. You'd better tell me what you're really here for, and quickly. Or you may find yourself in a worse state than Brice was when I finished with him.'

'I'm telling you the truth, chrono-san. I'm confessing to a crime. Shouldn't you be arresting me?'

Bullhammer lunged towards him, and pushed him to the ground. 'Don't you tell me how I should do my job, you little creep.'

Raffi looked up, dazed by the suddenness of the attack. He cowered from the policeman's raised boot.

'Tell me why you're here.'

Pain flared in his midriff as Bullhammer's toecap swung into him.

'Stop,' choked Raffi. He could scarcely breathe. Another kick, this time in the shoulder, sent him skidding across the shiny floor and clattering into the table leg. He felt brawny hands lifting him into the air, and a powerful smack across the mouth. The sharp taste of blood seeped into his throat. Then he was dropped ungently into his chair.

Bullhammer moved towards the exit. 'Perhaps you need

time to consider your answer. I'll be back in ten minutes. Try to come up with something a little more constructive this time.'

Raffi watched the giant-backed man press something on his belt. The door faded, he stepped through it, and Raffi was alone once more.

He toppled onto the floor and lay there for a while, eyes closed, trying and failing to get his thoughts to cohere into something like a plan. One of his front teeth felt distinctly wobbly. He was in the hands of a sadist, no question. Bullhammer would have his fun with him, and there was nothing Raffi could say or do to prevent that. Even confessing, it seemed, was not good enough. Opening his eyes, he looked around for some means of escape. But no window or ventilator grill broke the blank featurelessness of the walls and ceiling. The only access to the outside world was through that strange blue, melting door. Raffi rose painfully to his feet and walked over to it. He bashed it hard with his fist, achieving nothing more than a sore hand to add to his other injuries. Using the knuckles of his other hand he tapped on the wall in various places. Solid all the way through.

He couldn't simply wait for the brute to return. He had to do something. Raffi was tall, but not muscular like Dario, and was certainly no match for Bullhammer in a fight. Yet he was stronger than he looked. He had won a few bets beating bigger boys at school at arm wrestling. He was also quick. Maybe, just maybe, if he could take him by surprise…

He walked over to one of the chairs and picked it up. It was fairly heavy, but manageable. He lifted it over his head and swung it in an arc, nearly losing his balance as the weight and momentum of the chair toppled him forwards. Hoping fervently that no cameras were watching him, he carried the chair to one side of the door and took up a position next to it.

Now all he could do was wait…

CHAPTER TEN

⧖

THE UNDERSIDE

eavy footsteps sounded outside. Raffi tensed. He picked up the chair. The blue door disintegrated and Bullhammer strode in. Raffi didn't hesitate. He swung the chair in a rising arc and the front of its seat crashed into the police officer's face, causing him to stagger back through the still-open doorway. Seizing his chance before the man recovered, Raffi ran through the doorway and raced towards the exit. He heard a great roar behind him. 'Seal the exits!' Raffi glanced behind to see Bullhammer already back on his feet and charging towards him with giant strides. He was gratified to see, beneath the man's vengeful eyes, blood streaming from his nose. The exitway ahead slid shut with a hiss, extinguishing the light filtering down from the atrium above and with it, all hope of freedom. Raffi made a sharp turn to his left and sprinted down a corridor. The light turned blood-red and a siren sounded. 'Calling all personnel. Escaped detainee. Escaped detainee,' rasped a metallic voice. 'Currently travelling north along Corridor 3. Intercept using all available force.' Running footsteps were approaching along the corridor ahead, and he could sense Bullhammer gaining on him from the rear.

Raffi saw a door to his right: an ordinary door with a handle. He turned it and thankfully it opened. The room beyond was dark – too dark to see anything much once he'd shut the door. He flicked on his handcom light and saw in its green glow that he was in a store room full of boxes on shelves. On one of the shelves was a long black tubular shape, with a stock, a trigger and a sight – a dilator! He picked it up, just as the door behind him opened. A young police officer charged towards him. Raffi pulled the trigger, as he had seen Dario do, then turned the dial on the barrel to max. He felt a dull vibration and a cone of air enclosed the chrono-san, distorting the man's features like a reflection in a carnival hall of mirrors. The policeman slowed, his voice plunging to the deepest growl – then stopped. With his hands pawing the air in front, he looked like a stuffed bear in a museum. Raffi twisted the dial back to zero. Like power returning after an outage, the police officer's roar swelled to an audible pitch, and his limbs jerked back to life. He moved a few steps forward, then fell face down on the floor, knocked out by the temporal whiplash. Raffi quickly pulled off the man's boots, belt, trousers, jacket and shirt. Luckily, he was a similar build to Raffi. The trousers were a little on the short side, but otherwise the clothes were an okay fit. No one will notice the trousers, Raffi told himself, as he left the room and continued running north along the corridor. No one looks that closely.

'Halt!' yelled a voice behind him.

Raffi stopped, scarcely daring to turn. By now, surely, his face had been beamed to every police officers' handcom. A grey-haired senior officer with stars on his chest was staring at him.

'You seen Marv Bullhammer?'

'No.'

'Whose unit are you with, son?'

Raffi hesitated. 'Shep Tallis's unit.'

The man continued to stare. 'What is that on your face? Blood?'

'Yes, sir. Ran into someone earlier in the rush – when the sirens started up.' Raffi felt the sweat on his neck. His muscles were tensed to run.

The officer grunted. 'Listen, this escapee is dangerous. So if you see him, don't try and talk to him. Just use your incapacitator. Understood?'

'Understood, sir.'

'Right. Off you go.' He turned and marched away.

Raffi walked quickly in the other direction. Ahead lay a junction, and some signposts: Refectory, Restrooms, Reception, Interrogation Rooms, Desync Chamber, Re-Education Centre. Re-Education Centre! Maybe he would be able to find Dario there. The signpost directed him right, along a corridor that ended in a blue door. To open the other door, Bullhammer had pressed something on his belt. Raffi looked down and spied a small black protrusion with a recessed button near the buckle. He pressed it and, with a small hiss, the door dissolved to reveal a tiny glass room: a levitator. As soon as he stepped inside, the glass bubble began its silent descent into the darkness that lay beneath the upper dome: the mysterious Underside of the Chronosphere. Lights from far below revealed the space beneath his feet to be vast – yet he had the sense he was only seeing a very small part of the total area. At the bottom of the levitator shaft was a wide balcony, encircling a deeper space some twenty metres below it. A group of people in suits were gathered on the balcony, listening to a uniformed officer give a talk.

When it reached the level of the balcony, the levitator slowed and stopped and its glass door evaporated. Raffi stepped out. His boots made a satisfying echoing ring on the hard black floor as he marched purposefully towards the senior-looking officer addressing the group. Purposefulness was his only hope, he realised. Any suggestion of hesitation might arouse suspicion.

'Sir,' he announced loudly, interrupting the ginger-haired officer in mid-flow.

'Yes, what is it? Can't you see I'm busy?'

'I've been detailed to inform you that there is an escaped detainee inside the Police Centre, who may be dangerous. My orders are to guard this sector until he has been apprehended.'

'Yes, I heard something about that. Looks like you might have been caught up in it yourself. Is that blood on your face?'

'Yes, Sir.'

'Tell me, is the detainee desynchronised?'

Raffi had no idea what the man meant, but didn't hesitate in his response. 'I don't believe so, Sir.'

'Good, that should make things easier. Well, stick around, Chrono-San…?'

'Alephar Goddlea.' The anagram of Raffi's name sprang quickly to his lips. It had been his pen name when submitting controversial pieces for his school magazine.

'OK, Chrono-San Goddlea. I'm Chrono-Don Marcus Ripley. Just to fill you in, these good people are delegates from the 17th annual conference of the International Criminal Justice Foundation. They've come to learn a little about how we do things around here.' In a lower voice, he added: 'Let's try to be a little more discreet with our talk of escaped detainees, eh? We don't want people to get the wrong impression.'

'Understood, Sir.'

Raffi stood near the back of the group, as Ripley

continued his talk. 'Ladies and gentlemen, in a minute I'll let you see the cells. But since you may find this experience a little disorientating at first sight, I thought it better for you to meet a single inmate to start with. This man has been with us for five C-years now and is regarded as fully re-educated. In fact he is due to be released in just a few days' time, so you have nothing to fear from him. Please feel free to ask him anything you wish.'

Ripley spoke into his wearable, and a metal door at the far end of the balcony slipped into nothingness. A young man stepped out of the doorway and walked towards the group. He was tall and thin with long black hair swept back in a ponytail. His suit was several sizes too small, leaving his pale wrists and ankles on display. There was something else odd about him, though Raffi couldn't quite identify what.

The young man stopped several metres from the group.

He fixed on someone in the group, a fat man with a moustache. 'Very well,' he told him. 'They treat us –'

'How do they treat you here?' interrupted the fat man.

'– very well 'ere,' finished the inmate.

There was a confused silence. Then the inmate turned to a middle-aged woman near the back, and said: 'Watts. Septimus –'

'What is your name?' she asked, a horrified blush rising on her cheeks.

'– Watts is me name,' said Watts, completing his answer while she was still halfway through her question.

'Nineteen,' he said to a young man with rosy cheeks.

'And your age is?' asked the man, sounding flustered.

'Four,' Watts responded to a balding man near the front.

'What is two plus … two?' asked the balding man, tailing off slightly as he realized he had already been told the answer.

Watts looked over at Ripley and nodded: 'Yes, chronodon,' he said, and turned to leave.

'That'll be all, thanks, Septimus,' said Ripley. 'See you in a few days.'

Everyone stared as Watts retraced his steps towards the metal door. Watching him closely, Raffi now understood what he had found odd about the young man earlier. The sound of his footsteps bore no relation to the movement of his feet along the floor.

CHAPTER ELEVEN

⏳

Time-Shifted

'Extraordinary,' declared the fat man. 'Quite uncanny,' echoed the balding man. 'Desynchronisation,' explained Ripley. 'I predict that soon penal systems the world over will be adopting this system. Now, if you'd all care to follow me, we'll take a look at the men's section of what we call our Re-Education Centre. The women can be viewed, if you wish, later, but I assure you the set-up is identical.'

Ripley led the group to the edge of the balcony.

It took a little while for Raffi to make sense of what he was seeing. There were around twenty inmates in the well-lit, semi-circular area below him. The first thing Raffi noticed was that they were all young – none older than 18 or 19, a few as young as 14. Could these be the missing teenagers? Perhaps it was Secrocon that was kidnapping them? Maybe Dario had merely been working for them? No wonder Bullhammer didn't believe Raffi's confession. He knew the truth!

Poor kids! All they had was a bed and a wardrobe, a shower unit, sink and lavatory. Strangely, there were no walls dividing them, only white lines painted on the floor to demarcate the rectangular areas of each young inmate's territory. Despite the absence of walls, there was no interraction between the inmates. Each carried out their solitary activities – be it lying on their beds, washing, showering, reading, relieving themselves or exercising – uncaring or perhaps oblivious of their lack of privacy.

None of the observers commented on the youth of the inmates – perhaps they had been briefed what to expect. But someone did ask the other obvious question: 'Where are the cells?'

'Our Re-Education Centre requires no cells in the physical sense,' answered Ripley. 'Each inmate is in his own time-cell. When they are sentenced, they are desynchronised, or decoupled from the present moment, and cast adrift in time: for minor crimes, they may be shifted a few seconds or minutes into the future or the past, while the more serious crimes are punished with a more remote time slot. I wanted you to see Septimus because he had been shifted forwards by a few seconds. It would have been more difficult to comprehend what was happening in the case of a back-shifted inmate – you may have assumed he was just being slow. However, for obvious reasons, the vast majority of our inmates are back-shifted. As wardens, we obviously want to be ahead of the game, as it were.'

'But – but how?' stammered the rosy-cheeked young man. 'How do you move people back and forward in time like this?'

'Well, if you want a technical answer to that question, you'd better ask a physicist,' responded Ripley. 'But it's my understanding that the temporal engineers who developed the Chronosphere discovered a few interesting properties of time in the process. They discovered, for example, that time is like a field, similar to an electric or magnetic field, with two poles: the past and the future. 'Every part of the universe has its own local temporal field. Time on Mars, for example, is 3 or 4 minutes ahead of time on Earth. The Dezzy – that's our pet name for the desynchronization device – can create a personal time field by altering a person's psy-bi function. First they are dilated, or slowed in time, and then they are shifted forward or back.'

An older man spoke up. 'But if they're all in their own separate time zones, it must play havoc with meal times and sleep.'

'Good point,' said Ripley. 'Those are actually the only synchronised activities in the Re-Ed Centre. Everyone eats and sleeps at the same time, regardless of where they are on their personal body-clocks. The system works surprisingly smoothly. The inmates are aware of how their own timeslot relates to the present, but not how it relates to those around them, so fraternisation between inmates is all but impossible. They can announce things to each other, but they have no idea if or when what they have said will be heard or how it will be reacted to. The only persons with whom they can interract with any effectiveness are ourselves, the wardens. Because we know each inmate's timeslot, we can time our statements to them to make sure they hear them, and we also know when to listen out for their responses.'

'Why even bother with cell demarcations?' asked the balding man. 'Why not let them move around freely down there?'

'We did try that in the early days,' replied Ripley, 'but there were constant accidents as people kept bumping into other people who had occupied the same space a few minutes earlier or later, depending on their timeslot. We found it was safer, in the end, to keep them all separate – and the inmates actually prefer it that way.'

The middle-aged woman pointed at Raffi. 'That young man mentioned an escaped detainee earlier. Have you ever lost a desynchronised prisoner?'

Ripley smiled. 'Not yet. One of the great virtues of this system is that even if an inmate escaped, he would find it extremely difficult to operate out there in his time-shifted state, and would be instantly identifiable by anyone who met him.'

Raffi scanned the figures below, trying to pick out Dario. As he surveyed each inmate more closely, he noticed something else that marked them out besides their youth: it was hard to see the details from this distance, but as far as he could make out, they were all, in their own way, good-looking boys and young men. Although they differed in height and build, they were invariably healthy, strong and slim, with good bone structure, skin and hair. When Raffi finally spotted Dario, it was remarkable that even he, with his handsome profile and muscular build clearly evident in a tight-fitting singlet, didn't stand out in this particular crowd. He was lying on his bed, hands behind his head. Raffi approached Ripley and said quietly: 'With your permission, sir, I would like to check below in case our escapee has managed to infiltrate the cells.'

'I really don't see how that would be possible,' said Ripley. 'It's the most secure part of the entire sector.'

'Nonetheless, one can never be too careful.'

The officer smiled. 'I like your attitude, Chrono-San Goddlea. Go right ahead. You can use the levitator over there.' He pointed to the metallic doorway from where Septimus Watts had emerged earlier.

'Just one question before I go,' said Raffi. 'The doors in this building: are they time-shifted, too?'

'You're a bright young man,' beamed Ripley. 'Yes, when they're "opened", the whole doorway is actually shifted back to the time just before the doors were installed. Neat, isn't it?'

As Raffi marched away, an announcement came over the tannoy: 'All personnel be aware: escaped detainee is posing as a police chrono-san. All chrono-sans should report to their unit chrono-don on Level 1 immediately and present their biometric cards. No exceptions.'

Raffi quickened his pace.

'Hey, Chrono-San Goddlea!' It was Ripley.

Raffi was nearly at the door now. He pressed the black button on his belt. The door didn't open.

'Officer Goddlea!'

Raffi glanced back. He could tell Ripley didn't want to make a scene in front of the visiting delagates, but the man was evidently puzzled. His face was a giant question mark.

Raffi pressed the button again and, to his relief, the door shifted to its pre-existent state. He stepped in and it reappeared behind him. The levitator plummeted, and when the door disappeared again it revealed a ground-level view of the cells, with the nearest inmate just a few metres away. As Raffi emerged onto the concourse, he was approached by a security guard.

'Can I see your card please, chrono-san.'

They would all be on the lookout for the card of the man he was impersonating. Raffi had just seconds to work out what to do.

'Never mind about my card... Stamic,' he said sternly, reading the man's name badge. 'I have come here on the strict instructions of Chrono-Don Ripley to check on *your* details. The escaped detainee is strongly suspected of having infiltrated the cells, posing as a security guard.'

'But the announcement just now said he was posing as a police chrono-san,' argued Stamic.

'A clever piece of disinformation,' smirked Raffi, 'designed to make him think we were on the wrong track. Now can we go into your office? We haven't much time.'

The guard looked at him sceptically. 'Is that blood on your face, chrono-san?' he asked.

Raffi sighed. 'Yes. Now please can we go?'

He was led into a small, glass-fronted room containing a desk, a chair and a row of wall units.

Stamic's wearable sounded. The guard was about to respond when Raffi ripped the bleeping stud from his collar and spoke into it. 'Yes.'

'Stamic?'

It was Ripley.

'Yes.' said Raffi.

Before he could say any more, he felt a violent blow to his head and the stud fell with a small clatter to the floor. As he collapsed, Raffi heard Ripley's tinny voice coming through the stud's miniature speaker: 'There's a young man just arrived down there dressed as a police chrono-san and calling himself Goddlea. Arrest him please.'

'I've got him right here, sir,' said Stamic triumphantly.

Raffi, now on the floor, groped for a solid object and connected with the table leg. But as he began to raise himself up, he was kicked down again by Stamic. On his knees, he felt the handcuffs closing on his wrists.

'Take care now. He's highly dangerous,' said Ripley's voice. 'Use the incapacitator.'

Stamic unclipped a stubby black object from his belt and raised it towards Raffi's neck. Raffi braced himself.

But instead of the expected pain, he heard a sound of shattering glass. He looked up to see the entire window of the office caving in. It seemed to happen spontaneously, with no obvious cause. Startled, Stamic turned to see what had happened, and Raffi took the opportunity to whack the guard over the head with his handcuffed wrists. The blow knocked the man clean out, and he lay sprawled on the floor. Raffi looked up in time to see Dario diving through the space that had recently been occupied by glass. 'Dario,' he cried joyfully. Dario stood up, but his eyes were elsewhere and he didn't reply. He may have been watching Raffi whack Stamic. Or was he still watching Stamic kicking Raffi? There was no immediate way of telling how many seconds backward they'd shifted him. But such details would have to be worked out later. Guards would be swarming in here in a matter of seconds. 'Dario,' he cried. 'Get the key from Stamic and unlock these things.' He shook the handcuffs at him.

'Hey, Raffi, mate,' Dario said, sounding remarkably calm. 'That was very well done. Let me get you out of those cuffs.' He moved over to the motionless Stamic and removed the key from his belt. His fingers seemed clumsy with it, not out of nervousness, but something else. 'Damn desynchronisation,' Dario mumbled. 'It's hard to hold anything in this state. Everything feels rubbery, as if it's insulated from you.'

'How far back did they shift you?' asked Raffi, but Dario didn't answer. He was moving to a position near the table leg, where Raffi had been some seconds ago.

'Yes, yes. I'm going to,' said Dario. 'But hold still. I'm about 10 seconds behind you, so you must try to stay completely still while I do this.'

Raffi held still and waited, and eventually Dario's fingers collided with the metal surrounding Raffi's wrists, and managed, with a few false starts and one or two curses, to slide the key into place and release the cuffs. During the struggle, Raffi felt the brush of Dario's skin against his, or what should have felt like skin, but was something else quite different. It was as though Dario was wearing a glove of some ever-mobile substance; something almost like liquid, but not quite.

They had lost valuable time. Already he could hear guards approaching, though Dario could not.

'Come on, let's run for it,' he shouted, and tried to push

Dario away, but he couldn't be shifted. Where he existed, the cuffs were not yet unlocked. By the time they were, and Dario started to get up, they were surrounded by grey uniforms. One of the guards raised his dilator and Dario froze in its beam. Raffi would have been caught, too, had he not thrown himself to the floor. He crawled further into the room, into a dark corner where he found a door he hadn't spotted earlier. He pushed at it and to his great relief it opened. He slithered through, then scrambled to his feet. He was in a lavatory containing a urinal, a sink and a single cubicle: the cubicle would be the first place they would search. Looking up, he found what he was looking for. He climbed onto the sink, placing a foot on each side of it to give himself an unsteady perch, then grabbed the loose corner of a vent cover and pulled with all his strength. The cover ripped. Screws spilled and bounced into the sink. A few more tugs and it was free. He used his hands and knees to lever himself into the narrow opening, wriggling his way further into it just as he heard the lavatory door squeak on its hinges behind him.

CHAPTER TWELVE

⧗

Time-Twisted

The horizontal shaft was dark. It felt tight around him. But the metal was smooth and he could slip along it quite easily. After about two minutes of pushing, he saw a light up ahead, filtering through a mesh grille set into the right-hand side of the shaft. He caught the sound of a sob followed by a whimper from somewhere close by. He pushed his face close to the grille and found himself looking down on a brightly lit room containing three people – a grey-uniformed technician, a tall, distinguished-looking man with pale hair broken by a streak of black, and a very thin boy of about 15. The technician was pointing a gun at the boy, who was seated at a table. The strange-looking gun had a short, pinecone-shaped muzzle and an intricate arrangement of rods above the rear sight. A wide beam of pale pink light projected from its muzzle, enclosing the boy where he sat before a plate of delicious-looking food. To Raffi it looked and smelled like invitrocrabmeat on a bed of sea kale and samphire – one of his favourites. The boy had a forkful of the crabmeat hovering around six centimetres from his mouth. His eyes were bulging at the gorgeous sight of it and his arm muscles looked strained with the effort of moving it towards his mouth, yet he couldn't seem to bring the food any closer – or if he could, then it was by increments too tiny for Raffi to observe. The sobs and whimpers were being emitted by the boy, who was clearly starving and looked frustrated almost beyond reason that he couldn't eat. A string of saliva trailed downwards from his lower lip and hung beneath his chin. The distinguished-looking man was observing the boy closely from the other side of the room. 'Come on, young man,' he smilingly encouraged. 'Eat up now! What are you waiting for? It'll get cold soon.' These words made the boy cry out as if in physical pain. Unable to watch any longer, Raffi averted his eyes and crawled onwards.

A little further on, his hands found a side duct, narrower even than the one he was in. He squeezed himself into it, hoping that he wouldn't get stuck. With his arms now stretched in front, mole-like, he used his wrist muscles to propel himself by slow increments forwards. It was hard work, and his squashed lungs cried for more air. Ahead he saw dim light and this was what prevented him from giving up. Finally, his fingers met with another grille, and pushed. It was stuck fast. He pressed with desperate energy, but the cover held firm. As he stopped to gather breath, his eye was caught and held by the shadowy scene through the wire of the grille. A girl was sleeping in a bed in one corner of a large room. The furnishings of a bedroom combined with a bathroom were clustered in that corner. The rest of the room was an empty space.

As he watched, she slowly rose from the bed. She was wearing an old, shapeless green dress and her skin had the colourless quality of clothes that had been washed too often. And yet the dry lips, the blotchy skin, the unkempt hair couldn't mask a beauty in her face that held Raffi, even in his contorted state, enraptured. Her large brown eyes, though damp with tears, seemed to glow with a long-suppressed vitality; her mouth, though turned down at the corners, looked designed for impertinent and heart-warming smiles.

Her movements, however, were quite bizarre. Firstly, she walked backwards from the bed to the sink, and when she got there, she turned and bent towards it. Water flew up from somewhere – the plughole? – and into her mouth, then washed from her mouth into her hand and from there into the tap, which she promptly switched off. Then the girl moved to the toilet, which made a flushing sound until she pressed the button on the cistern, whereupon it stopped. She raised her dress and sat down. Raffi shut his eyes, not wanting to witness this most private of moments. When he opened them again, the girl was naked, facing away from him. She picked up a wet towel from the floor and rubbed it all over her body until every part of her skin was wet. Then she climbed into the bath just as a great spray of water rose up and drenched her. As she lay in the bath, Raffi saw tears on her cheeks slowly roll their way up into her eyes. He watched her unlather her legs and arms by running the soap backwards across them. Eventually she stood up, her body miraculously drying as she did so, and stepped out of the bath. A pile of underwear rose, as if conjured, from the floor to her hand.

It was only when she was decent again, in another shapeless dress, that Raffi was recalled to his own wretched situation. More in hope than expectation, he tried pressing the little black button on his belt. Incredibly, the cover in front of him shimmered, wobbled like a spider's web in a breeze, then vanished.

Hauling himself out of the shaft, he fell in a clumsy heap onto the floor below. Climbing to his feet, he approached the girl hesitantly, desperate not to scare her in case she screamed and alerted the guards. As she watched him approach she looked not scared but sad, almost tearful.

'Hello,' he said gently. 'I'm Raphael Delgado.'

The girl simply looked at him, her eyes full of sad regrets.

'Can you hear me?' he asked, wondering whether, because of her strange, back-to-front behaviour, they would be able to communicate at all.

She reversed to a small table near her bed and retrieved a pad and pen. He saw she had a bright red mark on her hand, like a burn. She was crying now. Her backward sobs sounded like odd, staggered exhalations. He thought he heard her say the word 'Anna'.

She handed the pad to him, with a pen. The page was full of her own jottings and he realised that this was the way they must communicate. Speech was useless. His words must sound like gibberish to her. Even facial expressions would make no sense when they were moving in opposite directions. Near the bottom of the pad he found a space to write: *Hello, I'm Raphael Delgado. What is your name?*

He handed the pad to her. She took it in her clumsy, reversed way: her grip moving from loose to tight as it would if she had been handing it to him. Then, shakily, she pointed to the words she had already written in answer to his question, on the line above.

He read: *Pleased to meet you? So then we must be near the beginning of our acquaintance. That means you will leave me soon. How very sad. But I must introduce myself: My name is Anna. It works backwards just as well as forwards. Handy for a girl in my state.*

She then pressed her nib to the final mark of this passage, and unwrote it back into her pen.

He didn't forget the words, though, even when they were gone from the page. For they were not a response to his last statement, but to the one he would now make.

Taking the pad, he wrote: *Hello Anna. I am pleased to meet you.*

Tearfully, she unwrote: *Do I? Thankyou. But could we really be friends? Even if we're contrariwise? It would be very confusing, don't you think?*

Raffi wrote: *I don't see why we can't be friends. You seem like a sweet girl.*

Her face gathered into a frown as she held up her next epistle:

Oh, I see. You've just answered the question I was about to ask. I'm sad we have such little time. I so wish, Raphael, that we could just move in the same direction for once, so that we could talk properly. Anyway, the question I was about to ask is: how long have we known each other?

Just a few minutes, Anna, he wrote – or his hand did. Raffi scarcely felt in control any more. Anna was determining his future by her messages, just as he was shaping her past with his.

She seemed more cheerful now. Her impish smile, with the jutting lower lip, enchanted him. Even her handwriting looked livelier: *So you think I am pretty!* was her next offering, hurriedly deleted.

Yes, I do, he wrote, amused. *I think you're very pretty.* Now did she plant that compliment, or had it come from him? These temporal paradoxes could be mischievous.

Her next message had a more serious tone, but she remained smiling: *Yes*, she had written, *they've cornered you. But don't be downhearted. Perhaps you will escape again from wherever you came from and come and visit me. Don't stay away too long, though, or I'll be too young for you!*

I should like that, he wrote. *Shall we make it a date? But I really don't want to leave here now. I like it here with you. And besides, I have no place further to go. I think they've cornered me like a rat.*

Raffi didn't say it, but he was also scared. Having witnessed the torture of the boy in the nearby room, he was more determined than ever to avoid capture.

No you won't. They will capture you, said she.

Don't worry about me. I'll be fine, he responded. He wished he really felt that confident. She, after all, had seen his future.

Anna held up the next message for him. The playfulness had gone from her now, replaced by a look of urgency. *I have been time-reversed*, she had written. *They flipped my temporal field. That's how I can see what will happen to you. For me, the future is no mystery, but the past is not yet formed. This past is different from the one I lived before. I never grew up in a prison cell, but now I'm growing down in one. You're the first person I've seen in I don't know how long. Can you get me out of here?*

I will try, he wrote back, meaning it.

She sat down on her bed, slipped under the covers. Now she looked sleepy, and the sense of urgency was draining away. The next message read: *Raphael: the angel of healing. You look like an angel. But can you heal me?*

I'll get you out of here first. Then I'll take you to someone who can help you. I'd like to be your friend. I'd like to get to know you better. I will return for you.

Anna looked groggy now, as if recently shaken from sleep. The red mark on her hand looked raw and painful. She slowly unwrote the top message on the pad, the first one she had written: *Who are you? Is your name Raphael?*

'Yes', he whispered. 'I am Raphael.'

There came a noise from outside the room. The guards were coming, as Raffi knew they would. He looked at Anna for perhaps the last and first time. She was now frightened, shrinking from him. He took her hand, the one with the mark on it. But her touch was like fire, like a friction burn on his fingers. He backed away from her, and saw that the mark had disappeared from her skin. Then he turned, just as the door opened and the guards surged in. One of them shone a spotlight into Raffi's eyes. 'There's the little bastard. Zap him.' Another one raised his dilator. Raffi ran straight at them, hoping against hope...

CHAPTER THIRTEEN

MEET DEZZY

The room faded and disappeared and was replaced by a completely white space. He might have been floating in a cloud, but for the solid presence of a man leaning over him. He felt light-headed, as though he'd taken one of Lastara's little pills. There was no fear.

The man had pale, almost white, blond hair with a flash of black that travelled through his left eyebrow and up the left side of his head. He wore a black robed uniform with the hourglass symbol slowly rotating on his chest. He smiled reassuringly. 'You're awake now. Good.' He had a warm, soothing voice and a handsome face. Raffi recognised him from an earlier scene involving a boy and some food. He didn't recall the scene too well now. He found himself wanting to trust the man.

'Where am I?'

'Desynchronisation Unit 5. You're nearly ready to meet Dezzy.' He made Dezzy seem like a wonderful new friend. 'We're just finalising your timeslot. It shouldn't be more than a few minutes. You just relax.'

Raffi found it quite easy to relax. The bed he was lying on was very comfortable. He ached all over: his fingers burned, his teeth hurt; his shoulder and knee and wrists were all suffering to varying degrees. But mentally he felt at ease. After all, he could hardly complain. He'd done wrong, hadn't he? He should never have assaulted Chrono-San Bullhammer, nor lied to Chrono-Don Ripley, nor hit the security guard Stamic. In fact, if he was honest, he'd been thoroughly disruptive and unpleasant all morning.

'Ah, here it is,' said the man, now reading from a screen. 'Two minutes, 48 seconds BS... That's short for back-shifted. And here's Dezzy.'

A large black machine hovered into view. It was a two-metre-long horizontal cylinder on a wheeled stand. On its side was a flat panel of flashing lights and buttons. The Dezzy was positioned so that one end of the cylinder faced Raffi's head. Then a grey-uniformed operator pressed one of the buttons and the cylinder split open at the bottom. The operator rolled it forwards so that Raffi's body was between the two half-cylinders. He heard it close beneath him with a click, and everything went black. Time passed – Raffi couldn't be sure how much. Then the cylinder opened a crack and light flooded in from below. Raffi soon found himself back where he'd been earlier, in the floaty white space being smiled at by the blond man.

'Welcome back, Raffi. Now that wasn't too painful, was it?'

Raffi shook his head, and the man stopped smiling and pressed a button on something that looked like a stopwatch. He nodded to one of the operators, then turned back to Raffi. 'Raffi, you've been backshifted 2 minutes and 48 seconds. I know exactly what you will say and do in the next three minutes, near enough. To put it another way, I am speaking from your future. I am Chrono-Sensei Avon Drak from Secrocon HQ. Chrono-San Bullhammer, Chrono-Don

Ripley and the security guard Stamic have informed me of your... activities this morning. You've been a busy lad. Are you now sorry for what you did?'

'Yes, Chrono-Sensei.'

'And you'll be a good boy from now on, won't you?'

'Yes, Chrono-Sensei.'

'That's good to hear. Well, as all seems to be well now, I shall hand you over to Chrono-Don Ripley. If you have any questions, you should refer them to him.'

The tall chrono-sensei departed as Ripley stepped forwards, wearing the expression of a mildly cross but good-natured schoolteacher. 'You managed to fool me good and proper, didn't you young man? But I'm glad to hear you've seen the error of your ways. Now, I can tell you that you are going to ask for some salve for your fingers, which we can provide. You will ask for food, which we can also let you have. Bear in mind, however, that the effects of these items will appear delayed from your perspective. People from your future will apply the salve and serve you food, but your body won't feel or taste these things until nearly three minutes have elapsed. Now, I will take you to your cell. Please follow me.'

Raffi rose slowly from his prone position and swung his legs down to the floor. As he did so, his body began to complain from all directions, chiefly from his fingers and stomach.

'My fingers are burning' he said, almost without meaning to. 'Do you have some cream? I'm also very hungry.'

Ripley looked at his watch. 'OK,' he said to the operators. 'I can head off now. I'll see you two later.' He walked through an archway and along a corridor. Raffi hobbled after him. He was feeling weak and it was hard to keep up. The floor beneath his feet seemed coated with something mobile, almost liquid. His fingers continued to burn. 'My fingers are really hurting,' he shouted.

Ripley looked at his watch, then called over his shoulder: 'That is what happens, I'm afraid, when you touch a time-reversed person. That young woman is in solitary confinement for a very good reason. You really have no one to blame but yourself.'

Raffi had to agree with that comment, but it didn't make the pain any easier to bear. They reached the hall with its inmates in their demarcated territories. To the left of Raffi's 'cell' was one belonging to a pale-skinned boy with a mop of blue-black hair, an aquiline nose and startlingly bright blue eyes currently fixed on a handcom game. The cell to his right was occupied by a book-reading lad with shoulder-length blond hair and a golden tan. Both ignored him, as they ignored each other, lost in their own times. He sat down on his bed. Without thinking about it, he had seated himself in an impression made by his future self in the mattress. On the table next to the bed was a plate containing four little domes of food, each a slightly different tone of pink or greenish grey. They were labelled 'sardine-on-toast sorbet'; 'parsnip jelly'; 'invitro-ham whip' and 'hot pear e'spuma'. He took a forkful of the ham one. It was coated in the same shiny element that covered everything in this new world. And it tasted of precisely nothing – future-ham – its flavour finally hitting his taste buds while he was eating the pear e'spuma.

Throughout the hall there was a constant background of disconnected mutterings, whisperings and occasional shouts. Despite these sounds, and the close proximity of bodies, it was a lonely place. A guard arrived with a tube of cream, which Raffi gratefully smeared on his sore fingers. Two minutes and 48 seconds later, he felt its cooling touch.

Raffi tried calling to the dark-haired boy to his right. The boy didn't respond. Blondy, however, stirred and looked up, but in the opposite direction. Some commotion in the hall must have attracted his attention, perhaps the shout that

Raffi had heard a quarter of an hour ago, or maybe one he was about to hear: there was just no way of knowing where in time the boy was. He followed Blondy's stare and saw a young man nursing a bloody forehead.

Raffi decided he should pay a visit to Dario, who he could see on the far side of the hall. If they couldn't actually communicate, he could at least show him he was alive and well. He walked down the aisle that led from his cell to the edge of the hall. About halfway along he collided with something solid, yet invisible. Raffi staggered back, clutching his nose. Then he saw, sitting on a nearby bed, the young man with the bleeding forehead. 'I'm sorry,' he said, pointlessly.

He continued on his way, more carefully this time. Dario was lying on his bed, his muscular arms on prominent display with his hands clasped behind his head. He already had his eye on Raffi. 'You finally got here,' whispered Dario, looking at a space a little way to Raffi's left. 'Just stay exactly where you are and don't move, and we'll be able to talk. Act as if we're not, though. Look away from me while you're talking... That's it. That way they won't notice anything.'

'How can we do this?' asked Raffi.

'I saw you bump into the bloke back there and I happen to know his timeslot. From there it was an easy calculation to make. They back-shifted me further after our escape attempt. Turns out we're only a couple of seconds apart.'

'You okay?' asked Raffi.

'Just peachy,' said Dario. 'Listen mate, we tried. At least we tried.'

Raffi frowned. He didn't understand Dario's attitude. 'There was nothing clever about what we tried to do,' he told him. 'We shouldn't have tried to escape. We're here because we deserve to be, because we've done wrong.'

Dario looked sad. 'Oh Jeebus! They've got to you, haven't they? Yeah, they got to me, too, for a while. Listen, Raffi.

Don't touch the parsnip, okay? It's drugged. The rest of the grub's clean. If you stay off the parsnip for a day or so, you'll start to think clearly again.'

Raffi was unhappy to hear these words from his friend. Rehabilitation was clearly some way off for him. 'If you keep up that rebellious attitude, Dario, it'll be a long time before they let you out of here.'

Dario chuckled quietly. 'You still think they let anyone out of here? You got to be kidding, mate. Everything Sal ever said about this place is true. Actually it's even worse than she imagined. It may seem like paradise up there, with the perpetual sunshine and the days by the lake. But it's actually a police state. The reason why it's so sweet and bland all the time Topside is because the minute anyone tries to do anything different or unusual, it's out with the dilator and down they come to this place.'

'You mean like kidnapping someone,' said Raffi, angry now.

'I didn't kidnap anyone. You saw it wrong.'

'That girl went into the store, you took one look at her, pulled out your dilator, and zap. I saw it all, Dario. You don't have to lie to me.'

'You saw it wrong, mate. That's all I can say.' He gestured to the other cells, then whispered: 'if anyone's kidnapping kids around here, it's Secrocon.'

Raffi felt deeply disappointed: he had hoped that by confronting Dario he would at least extract some acknowledgement of guilt, but there was not even a flicker of remorse or regret in Dario's eyes. Instead he preferred to indulge in ridiculous conspiracy theories. Raffi was no longer certain he could even be friends with such a person. 'Well, see you later,' he said, with as much amiability as he could muster.

'Remember,' whispered Dario. 'Don't touch the parsnip.'

Raffi walked slowly back to his cell. He lay down on his bed and stared up at the balcony above them, and the dim, mysterious reaches beyond. He missed his domicile in Time Tower; his balcony view; his hoverbike. He even missed Flora. More than all that, he missed Jonah. He hoped that one day, once he was fully rehabilitated and could return to the Topside of the Sphere, that he and Jonah could put their differences behind them and go back to being best friends.

At a certain moment, some indefinable amount of time later, the lights illuminating the hall suddenly switched off and they were plunged into complete darkness. The background hum of whispers and mutterings continued, unaffected by this abrupt change: only Raffi, after all, experienced the switch at that particular moment. Gradually, the noises diminished and, if not silence, then a kind of hush, descended. His last thought before sleep overtook him was of the sad, time-reversed girl in her lonely room somewhere not far from here. Was she thinking of him? He had rashly promised to save her – but that was before he had understood that she, like he, was here for her own good. If they were ever to meet again, it would be Topside, once they had both served their time and were fully rehabilitated. He hoped that day would not be too long in coming.

CHAPTER FOURTEEN

GOING UNDERGROUND

Raffi was awoken by a nudge on his shoulder. He opened his eyes and was surprised to see Dario crouching there in the gloom by his bedside. 'Listen mate,' whispered Dario. 'Keep quiet. We're going to get out of here.'

Raffi tried to sit up. 'What?' he said. 'Are you crazy?'

'Shhh! Listen. We're being rescued.'

'No, Dario. I don't want to be rescued. I must stay here, and you must, too. We're here for our own good, remember. Besides, the security's too tight. Escape is impossible.'

'I'd agree with you about the security,' said Dario. 'If we were trying to head upwards.'

'What are you talking about?'

Dario pointed to the ground. Next to where he was squatting, a large floor tile had been removed, revealing a black rectangular hole. 'Come on!' he beckoned. Raffi was sure he was dreaming as he watched Dario's bulky figure begin to disappear through the hole.

'I'm going to have to tell the guards about this,' warned Raffi.

Dario looked saddened by this. 'Listen, mate. If you don't want to come, that's fine. But don't dob me in for a second time. That's not what being mates is all about.'

With that, he disappeared through the floor. Raffi stared into the abyss. 'I suppose I'd better close it up,' he thought. 'I don't want the guards to think I had anything to do with this.' He was about to get out of bed to do so when Dario reappeared. He reached out an arm and grabbed Raffi's exposed ankle, hauling him down. Raffi nearly cried out. His hand reached out to grasp something, anything, to prevent himself from falling. It closed around the rim of the hole, but Dario pulled him further and then held him tightly around the chest.

'Sorry, mate,' said Dario, dragging the floor tile back into place with his other hand. 'I just couldn't bear the thought of leaving you up there.'

A bright light switched on below them, and the shock of this caused Raffi to shout out. Dario jumped at this sound and dropped Raffi, who promptly fell downwards, straight into the light. He heard a shattering of glass, then all went black.

Raffi awoke some while later. He was in a dark place with a low ceiling and walls of blue-black brick. A young man was looking down at him. He was unshaven and his filthy hair was pulled back in a ponytail. Raffi was sure he'd seen him somewhere before, looking a lot cleaner and tidier.

'Hey Raffi!' grinned the young man. 'You're awake!' He had a couple of missing teeth and didn't exactly look a picture of health. 'I'm Septimus Watts, your rescuer.' He handed him an old chipped mug. 'Water?'

Raffi drank gratefully, then wiped his mouth. 'Weren't you the inmate that Ripley was showing off to those delegates?'

'I believe I may 'ave been, yeah.'

'How come we can talk?'

'Cos I shifted you back to normal time. Rigged up me own version of Dezzy, din't I? I call her Rezzy – for Resynchronizer. She's a'right, but not perfick. If you start gettin' strange visions, they're probably just little flashes from the future. But don't worry too much 'bout it – unless you get one of yerself in a small wooden box!'

'Is this a vision now?'

'Nah, chum!' he chuckled. 'This is present reality. 'Fraid you're stuck with this one.'

Memories began to return. Raffi recalled a recent time when he'd felt very contented with his lot as an inmate of the Re-Education Centre, aware that he'd done wrong and that he must be punished. He no longer felt that way. Now he was glad to be out of there. The Re-Ed Centre had been full of kids of his age and even younger. How could he have possibly believed that was alright? He also recalled the hungry boy who'd been tantalised with food then denied it. What sort of place were they running here?

'Where are we?' he asked Septimus.

'I call it the Lower Warren, Raffi. Bin comin' down here nights for over a year now. Guards don' even notice. Far as they're concerned, the pile of pillows under me blanket is me snorin' away. It all started when I accidentally found a shaft under the floorboards of me cell. Found others, too – includin' the one under your cell. They all led down to this huge maze of abandoned tunnels. No idea what they were built for. One of 'em led to a machine shop full of parts. I used 'em to build the Rezzy and a couple of other 'andy little gadgets. Now, everythin's ready, I can escape for good, can't I? No more creepin' back to me cell before dawn. And you and Dario don't need to go back neither.'

'But they're going to come looking for us, aren't they? When they see our beds empty, they'll find that hole beneath my floor soon enough.'

'Filled up all the shafts last night, din't I? And we won't be missed anyways.'

'How come?'

'Follow me, I'll show ya.'

Raffi rose wearily to his feet. He was hungry – an almost perpetual feeling in the Sphere, and also a bit bruised and shaky. He followed Septimus into a narrow corridor lit by a single lightbulb, and then into another room. The dark, dingy brickwork was depressingly ubiquitous. Everywhere was cramped, as though built for a race of subterranean dwarves. A large and ramshackle machine dominated the room. Septimus stroked its flank like a proud father. 'This,' he said, 'is the Volumetric Parallax Panoramagram Display Device – Veepod for short. It makes perfick replicons of any object inside a synthesised 3-D light field. I scanned you and Dario last night, then placed replicons of both of you in your cells upstairs.'

Raffi gulped. 'Replicons – made of light?'

'Yes indeedee!' Septimus gave another delighted, gap-toothed grin.

'Well, that's hardly going to fool them, is it? I mean the minute one of the guard touches one of us…'

'They never touch yer, 'aven't you noticed? You're time-shifted, which means you're insulated from the world by a thin layer. You must've seen it on the surface of everythin' after you came outta the Dezzy? Touchin' a time-shifted person is never very nice, and guards don' like doin' it. They'll use their dilators on anyone misbehavin.'

'Misbehaving? But my replicon won't be capable of any kind of behaviour, good or bad, will it?'

'That's where you're wrong, Raffi, old chum,' chortled Septimus. 'That is where you are so wrong. See, this Veepod don't just create light-statues, it creates semi-autonomous functioning light-individuals. My ultimate plan is to build a

Hyperfunctional Magnetic Resonance Imager that can scan yer mind and then implant yer personality into the Veepod. Then I really could produce perfickly credible copies of anyone. Until that day, I've imbued 'em with default personalities.'

'Default…?'

'Yeah, your replicons are just a couple of dull geezers, who, y'know, sit around, sleep, read, scratch their bums, that sort of stuff. They won't win any prizes for charisma, but as it goes, that might not be such a bad thing, as there's zero chance of either of 'em attracting undue attention.' He ushered Raffi through a doorway at the far end of the room and into another corridor. 'The crucial thing is that your biometrics check out: iris, retina, voice, fingerprints – and all of those 'ave been carefully copied by the Veepod.'

'Do you really think it'll fool the guards?'

'It already 'as. You saw that one of me upstairs, din't you?'

'That was a replicon?'

'Yeah, course it was! And now Ripley's showin' it off to visitin' dignit'ries as an example of a model inmate, so you tell me – if that's not proof of success I dunno what is.'

The corridor bent sharply to the left and opened out into a better-lit area with a wooden table, a sink and some hastily constructed shelves and cupboards. Dario was there, putting something into the gastrovac cooker.

'Hey, good to see you, mate!' he greeted Raffi. 'Fancy some breakfast? We've got invitro-bacon fritters with vanilla ice-cream.'

Raffi, nearly keeling over with hunger, could have kissed Dario then and there, but he barely reciprocated Dario's warm greeting – still unsure how he felt about him, and not knowing what to believe about his role in the kidnappings.

After they had tucked in, he asked Septimus where the food had come from.

'Dug a tunnel to the prison stores, din't I?' replied Septimus. 'The replicons don' eat, so it all balances out an' no one's the wiser.'

'You are nothing short of brilliant,' declared Dario, clapping Septimus on his scrawny back. 'Don't you think so, Raffi? Our friend Septimus has single-handedly created a self-sustaining world down here. And through his mechanical genius, he's been able to engineer the perfect escape. I want to thank you, Septimus, for choosing to take us with you.'

Septimus nodded as he chewed on a fritter. 'I saw what you two tried yesterday. I liked your spirit, tryin' to escape like that. I said to meeself then, I said: if I make my escape tonight, I'm takin' those two with me.'

'But why even try to escape?' queried Raffi. 'Ripley said you were about to be released anyway.'

'Ripley said that, did he, the sly old fox! You should know one thing about that place up there, Raffi,' he said with a glance to the ceiling, 'no one ever leaves. It ain't a system of justice they're running there. It's a gulag.'

Raffi recalled the tortured boy he'd seen, and poor, time-twisted Anna. 'But what are they doing here exactly?' he asked. 'I thought this was supposed to be a pleasure resort, not a torture centre. And all of them just kids, like us.'

'Torture?' gulped Dario. 'Who said anything about torture?'

'I saw some things while I was on the run,' said Raffi. 'A hungry boy was being denied food…'

'I dunno,' shrugged Septimus. 'Maybe they don't like kids… What I do know is that this place ain't a pleasure resort – that's not its real purpose. They're kidnapping those kids for a reason. And what we've seen up there is prob'ly just the tip of the iceberg.'

'What do you mean?'

'They call this place the Chronosphere, right? Which

means it's a sphere. We know how big the top 'alf is: it's at least six kilometres across and over a kilometre high. The underground part must be the same size or even bigger, but we've only seen the central core: the Police Centre and the Re-Ed Centre below it. What about the rest? They could be holdin' thousands of people in the Underside and we wouldn't know a thing about it!'

'A gulag,' whispered Raffi.

'Voilà!'

'But how does the Time Store think it can get away with this?'

'I dunno if the Time Store even knows about this. The time differential between the Sphere and the outside world is so great, it 'as to be run as a separate operation. The Sphere's basically under the control of Secrocon and its top man, the Chronomaster. Some say 'e's gone a bit power mad. No one can say for sure 'cause few people ever get to meet him.'

'But eventually people will start to wonder where their loved ones are and come looking for them.'

'Mebbe that's why they're pickin' on kids. Dunno if you noticed, but the Sphere's full of runaway teens, escapin' parental authority – perfick targets for Secrocon cos no one'll notice they're missin' for ages.'

Dario began clearing the dirty plates. 'So how do we get Topside again?'

'There's a shaft I found leadin' to the surface not far from 'ere. Course there's no point goin' up there now, cos they'll only catch you again and send you back for more punishment. Mebbe even torture, if what Raffi says is right. The only foolproof way of escapin' is to get a new identity, includin' a new set of biometrics. An' that is somethin' I can help you with.'

'What about you? Aren't you coming with us?'

'Nope.' Septimus picked at something stuck between his

teeth. 'That was my plan once, but my world is down 'ere now. See, the more I've explored, the more curiouser I've got. I wanna find out where all these tunnels lead. I'm creatin' this map, buildin' up a picture of the Underside. I wanna find out where they're keepin' the other inmates, if there *are* other inmates. And I wanna find the heart of the Chronosphere – Secrocon HQ.'

⧗

CHAPTER FIFTEEN

STORM AND ELLIS

After breakfast, Septimus took Raffi and Dario on a little wander around the Lower Warren. To Raffi, it seemed endless, with a ridiculous number of similar-looking rooms and corridors forming a gigantic, pointless labyrinth.

'What are these white arrows on the walls?' he asked.

'It's very easy to get lost,' Septimus explained. 'I marked the walls so I'd always know how to get back to base.'

'Do you know where you are in relation to the prison above?'

'Worked a lot of it out by pacin' it out on the prison floor during days. Guards sometimes wondered what I was doin', but mostly left me alone. Transcribed it to me map each night.'

'Do you know where the girl's prison is?'

Septimus nodded. 'Why d'ya wanna know?'

'There's a girl,' Raffi said. 'I can't tell you exactly where she is, but…'

'You wanna rescue her, is that what you're askin'?'

'You're a dark horse,' laughed Dario. 'You had the entire

police and security forces on your tail, and you managed to find time to start a romance.'

'Well, not exactly, but…'

'Can ya tell me roughly where she is, Raffi?'

'If you show me your map, perhaps I can work it out.'

Septimus led them to his study. He'd masked the bleak brick walls with roughly built shelves lined with rows of ancient print-books. In the middle of the room was a large table of thick, gnarled timber. In a clear space on the table surface he unfurled his map. Raffi was immediately impressed with the level of detail and the precision of the draftsmanship. Each line and letter had been inked with meticulous care.

The map showed the floor plan of the Re-Education Centre and, alongside it, an equal-scaled map of the Lower Warren. The Re-Ed Centre map showed the men's and women's cells, guards' quarters, desynchronisation units, storage rooms and administrative offices. There were blank areas containing pencilled question marks, and a large blank margin of about 30 centimetres width all round the map's edge.

'As yer see, I've 'ardly started,' admitted Septimus. 'There are places even within the known prison that I don't know nothin' about – secret rooms, corridors and stuff. And beyond the prison boundary…' he gestured to the blank spaces at the edge of the map. 'I'm like an ancient mariner, ain't I? Tryin' to chart the world's oceans. I may as well write "'Ere be dragons".'

Raffi studied the map. He located the office where Stamic had taken him, and then the bathroom behind it. 'There's a ventilator shaft running along here,' he said, tracing a line with his finger from the bathroom. 'I must have gone about thirty metres or so when I saw the side-duct that led to her room. What's thirty metres at this scale?'

''Ere,' said Septimus, pointing to a place next to one of the bare, question-marked areas. 'Raffi old chum, you may just 'ave helped me fill in one of me blanks.'

'Can we tunnel up there?' asked Raffi.

'No fear. Not durin' the day. Maybe tonight though.'

'There is one other thing…' Raffi hesitated.

'What is it, mate?' asked Dario.

'The thing is, she's… time-twisted.'

'Whaddya mean?'

'Well, as far as I can tell, she's living her life backwards. Her movements and speech are all back-to-front, and her whole perception of time is the opposite of ours.'

'Time-reversed?!' Septimus's eyes looked like they were about to pop out of his head. 'I've 'eard rumours of that. But I never believed 'em. It breaks a cardinal rule of physics, don't it? – Second Law of Thermodynamics. That's the law that explains why cups of tea cool down and why balloons burst if you prick 'em. Localised energy disperses, see? 'Appens all the time, throughout the universe. For your time-reversed girlfriend, energy would 'ave to move in the other direction: from dispersed to localised. Burst balloons would reinflate, smashed windows would reassemble 'emselves. It just never 'appens.'

'Well that is what I saw,' said Raffi. 'Unless you're suggesting that she had mastered the art of walking and talking backwards, and of getting water to flood out of a plughole into a tap, or spring up at her as she stepped into a bath.'

'You saw her taking a bath?' said Dario, impressed.

'Yeah – backwards.'

'Either way would suit me!'

Septimus shook his head sceptically. 'I just can't see 'ow they could reverse time's arrah.'

Raffi tried to recall what Anna had told him. 'She said they managed to... flip her temporal field, whatever that means.'

This caught Septimus's interest. He went over to his bookshelf, and took down a fat, red-spined tome. 'Temporal fields?' he muttered, leafing through the pages. This book was written by a physics professor I knew called Astra Hitherbee. I always thought she was a bit of a fruitcake, but...' He stopped on a particular page. 'She says 'ere that time is a bipolar, non-inverse field.' He looked up. 'Bipolar means it 'as two poles, past and future. Non-inverse means that as the field lines draw closer, the field strength increases, makin' it more difficult to run against – which is why time moves in just the one direction, from past to future.' Septimus scratched his head. 'If 'er theory is correct,' he muttered, 'I s'pose it might be possible to run against a local temporal field and move someone and their immediate surroundings from the future... into the past. I dunno. At one point I think she speculates...' he flipped through more pages. 'Ah, here we are. She says that field strength may depend on density of time. See, she 'ad this theory that time is quantal, like grains of sand in a given space, and you could 'ave diff'rent densities of time, like diff'rent densities of sand. Maybe in a place of great time-density, like the Chronosphere, time reversal might be possible... All speculation o' course.'

'Well, whatever the cause of her condition, do you think we'll be able to rescue her?'

Septimus shook his head gravely. 'If she's time-reversed, I don't see how we can interrack with her on a physical level. Did yer try touchin' this girl?'

Raffi nodded and showed them the burns on his fingers, which had started to blister.

'Well then you know better than any of us that a rescue is completely impractical. Whatever pain you felt with that touch, I'll bet she felt its equal. It's obvious she can't be touched, or moved from her immediate environment. Nah, before we do anythin' else, we need to find a way of flippin' 'er temporal direction.'

'I'm sorry Septimus, mate,' said Dario, 'but this time-reversal thing is doing my head in. Are you saying that her life is in rewind mode and all her experiences are happening again in reverse order?'

'No,' said Raffi. 'That can't be right because I've never met her before.'

'So, what you're saying is that you can have different pasts, just like you can have different futures, depending on the choices you make? Nothing is fixed – in either direction?'

'Well, yes and no,' said Raffi. 'Some strange things began happening during our conversation. Because we were moving in opposite directions relative to each other, her responses seemed to be determining my questions, and vice versa. It was odd how I felt almost compelled to say certain things – to voice the questions that she had already answered.'

'So what happens eventually?' asked Dario. 'She keeps getting younger and younger until what, her mum mysteriously appears from somewhere and sucks her up inside her?'

'Nah,' said Septimus. 'I reckon when the baby gets too feeble to support itself outside the womb, Secrocon could find a willin', time-reversed surrogate mum to carry the foetus back to embryo and then, ultimately, to nothing. Or else they could leave the foetus to die outside the womb. But if I know Marcus Ripley, I doubt they'll take 'er back that far.'

'What do you mean?'

'Well, my guess is that this girl may 'ave done something they din't like. Now they wanna take her back to a time before she did this "crime", before even the thoughts and feelin's that led 'er to do it 'ad started to form. When she reaches that stage, they'll flip 'er back to a normal time flow and see what 'appens. She's an experiment. And maybe not the only one.'

Poor Anna, thought Raffi helplessly.

Dario pointed to a square near the bottom of the map, south of the Re-Ed Centre boundary. 'What's that?'

'That,' said Septimus, 'is your escape route, chum. As soon as I've given you your new identities, you'll be able to use it.'

Receiving new biometric data wasn't going to be easy or pleasant. Fingertips had to be filed down and the raw skin moulded into new prints; vocal cords had to be stretched and distorted, and laser surgery was required to alter irises and retinas. Septimus showed Raffi and Dario the surgical apparatus he'd painstakingly assembled from parts stolen during secret trips to the prison hospital. Raffi felt physically sick just looking at the torture chamber of black padded seating, robot arms, scalpels, facemasks and metal clamps. It didn't help to hear Septimus's cheerful admission that he was a complete beginner when it came to the medical arts. 'Still,' he added with an attempt at reassurance, 'can't be too hard this surgery lark, can it?'

Fortunately, Septimus had also found himself a high-quality anaesthetic. Raffi awoke from a period of such all-enveloping blankness that it took him a few seconds to recall himself. He couldn't see a thing and his first terrifying thought was that he'd gone blind. Panic seized him.

'It's alright, chum,' came Septimus's consoling voice. 'It's only the bandages on your eyes. They'll be off in a jiff, along with the dressings on your hands and neck.'

He tried to speak, but only a whisper emerged: 'How did it go? Will I survive?'

He had to be comforted by Septimus's cackle of laughter.

The first-time surgeon hadn't exaggerated about the speed of recovery. On one of his prison hospital raids, he'd found a stash of hyperbaric chrono-domes – miniature chronospheres, just 15 centimetres in diameter, that could be placed over surface wounds to speed up the healing process. Within an hour the bandages could be removed from Raffi's eyes.

The first sight for his brand-new peepers was Dario, looking weak and pale, but upbeat as ever. 'Welcome back to the world, mate,' he said in a hoarse, unfamiliar voice. 'How the devil are you?'

It may have been the new eyes, Raffi couldn't be sure, but seeing Dario's big, warm smiling face just then, he suddenly knew there couldn't be a bad bone in his body. And whatever he'd seen or thought he'd seen that day on Tomorrow and Third couldn't change the fact. He grinned back at him. 'I'm good thanks, Dario.'

Septimus, it turned out, had done a grand job. There were no visible scars on either of them and it was almost impossible to see they'd been tampered with. Dario's voice sounded deeper and richer, almost like a singer's. And his eyes were a paler blue with no more flecks of brown. Raffi's voice sounded huskier to his ears. His formerly pale brown irises had gone much darker.

Septimus gave them their new identities. 'Raffi, your new monicker is Michael Storm. Dario, you're Christo Ellis. I got the names and biometrics from my Topside source, a bloke called Parsim Pennyminder. 'E runs the cosmetic enhancement store at the top of the escape shaft. 'E's also an accomplished 'acker, who managed to get past the Secrocon cybershields to access their customer database. According to Parsim, this pair left the Sphere about two weeks ago. 'E's deleted records of their departure, so they're still officially resident. It's perfick! You'll 'ave access to their bank accounts, and you'll both be out of the Sphere well before they notice anythin' – so you can reimburse 'em then.'

At that moment, all hell broke loose. Four prison guards in grey uniforms suddenly charged into the room. They seemed to arrive without warning – an ambush. Raffi, Dario and Septimus were already running, but too slowly for the guards, and Raffi saw one of them bash Septimus on the head with a metal stick. Another fired an incapacitator at Dario, sending him tumbling. A third raised a dilator towards Raffi, and then the scene dissolved into swirling grey clouds.

Raffi found himself standing once more in the room with Dario and Septimus. Nothing had changed from a few seconds ago. Dario was calmly listening to Septimus as he told them about their new identities. 'Septimus,' Raffi interrupted. 'I've just had a very strange waking dream. Four security guards burst in here and clobbered us.'

Septimus looked up. 'Oh Jeebus!' he cursed. 'You've 'ad a Rezzy Flash! It's a fault in the Rezzy: it sometimes gives you short visions of the future. It means we've got two minutes and 48 seconds before what you saw actually 'appens.' He pondered. 'They must've wised up to those replicons and found what's left of the shaft under Raffi's cell. You two'd better get goin'… This way now. Scoot, scoot.' He began herding them down a southward corridor.

'But if it's the future, it's going to happen anyway,' said Raffi despairingly. 'We can't change it.'

'You can 'ave diff'rent futures,' averred Septimus. 'It's like what Dario said – depends on the choices you make. Nothing is fixed… Now come on, we need to move faster.'

'What about you?' asked Dario.

'Don't sweat about me. They'll never find ol' Septimus in all these tunnels. I'm the one with the map, remember!'

After leading them through about a dozen identical-looking rooms and corridors, Septimus stopped and indicated above their heads to a dark hole punched through the low ceiling: the opening of the escape shaft. Behind them, they heard muffled shouts and the scuffle of running footsteps. 'There 'ere,' he whispered. 'Thank Bo for your Rezzy Flash, Raffi, or we'd all be dead meat by now. Now, quick, get yourselves up there.'

'Where should we go once we're out?' asked Raffi.

Septimus hurriedly told them their new domicile numbers. 'Your MAID is Brigitte, Raffi. And Dario, yours is Mandy. I never got character profiles for your new identities, so you'll just 'ave to feel your way into the roles.'

The footsteps were getting closer.

'Thanks for everything, Septimus,' said Dario, clasping the young man's thin shoulder.

'Yeah, we won't forget what you've done for us,' added Raffi.

'Okay, okay. Now scat, the both of you.'

Raffi went first, stepping onto a table and using a pair of iron pegs at the lip of the opening to haul himself upwards. The shaft was narrow – so much so that his shoulders rubbed against its sides as he mounted the pegs that protruded from the concrete. There was no beckoning gleam of daylight at the top. He heard Dario clamber up beneath him. For a long while they climbed upwards in silence, until the illuminated room below them was just a pale circle of light no bigger or brighter than a five u-doll coin. Finally, that too became lost somewhere below Dario's bulk, and all was darkness and heavy breathing. Raffi stopped for a rest, pushing his feet against the pegs and leaning his shoulder against the shaft wall. 'How much further can it be?' he wondered.

'These pegs are set about half a metre apart,' murmured Dario, 'and we've climbed 86 of them – can't be much further now.' Even the air-tennis and wave-riding jock sounded breathless. 'Just think about that cool glass of Alligator I'll buy you,' he added.

'Assuming the police aren't waiting for us at the top,' said Raffi.

'Crikey mate, if I'd wanted that sort of comment, I'd have invited Sal along.'

After several more spurts of energetic climbing, Raffi's head clunked against something heavy. He pushed at it and it moved. Cold dust fell onto his hair and face, causing him to cough, and his still-sensitive eyes to run.

'Hold it a moment,' he spluttered, dropping the trapdoor so he could wipe his eyes. Then, with both hands, he heaved upwards and the door rose with a reluctant groan before falling open with a crash.

Raffi clambered out, then gave Dario a hand up. They were in a cellar. Stacks of plastic crates gleamed palely in the faint grey light from a half-open doorway at the top of a stone stairway.

After shaking the last of the dust from his hair and clothes, Raffi led the way up the stairs and cautiously pushed open the door. He blinked in the unaccustomed light, and drew in a deep lungful of clean air. They were in a retail unit – Parsim Pennyminder's cosmetic enhancement store. The unit's longest wall was lined with a row of holographic heads with constantly altering features: noses, eyes and mouths grew, shrank and changed shape, complexions lightened and darkened and hair changed style and colour in myriad ways. The store was empty of people, save for the man Raffi assumed to be Parsim, a thin, balding individual who was standing behind a counter, his fingers pecking away at a small computer. Dario gave him a smile and a small half wave, but Parsim did no more than look at them, blink once slowly, then return to his work. He was a pro, thought Raffi. He knew who they were, but he also knew not to acknowledge the fact.

They looked through the store's transparent frontage.

Outside, Fleeting Avenue bustled with early-afternoon pedestrians. Raffi and Dario stared at them and at the warm, ersatz sunlight that filtered down between the branches of the trees. How long had it been? No more than three days as convicts and then fugitives underground – but it felt like weeks.

'OK, Michael,' murmured Dario.

'OK, Christo.'

'Let's go.'

They pushed open the door and let the warmth and light flood their bones.

CHAPTER SIXTEEN

⏳

DARIO'S STORY

efore going to their domiciles, the boys headed to Atomic Sands for the glass of Alligator they'd promised themselves. 'Have you noticed how warm it is?' said Raffi, as they walked through Periodic Park towards the lakeside bar.

Dario nodded. 'Nice to see girls dressed in so little,' he commented, eyeing a group of young women.

'Jonah'll be happy. He always complains he's too cold.'

Jonah.

The thought struck them both at the same time. How would they explain to Jonah, Sal and Lastara that they were now different people, and that no reference must ever be made to their previous identities?

'Sàl will understand immediately,' said Dario. 'All this cloak-and-dagger stuff is meat and drink to her. We'll have to be more careful with the other two. I don't know if Lastara will want to have much to do with me now, anyway.'

'I heard about your break-up,' said Raffi, trying to be tactful.

'It was tough, but I had to do it.'

'She told me she gave you the push.'

Dario laughed. 'That's just Lastara's pride. In her way of thinking, no one could ever give Lastara Blue the push. It's inconceivable. So she just rewrites history.'

'I see,' said Raffi, keeping his voice neutral. 'Anyway – young, free and single, eh?'

'That's me.' Dario didn't sound too chirpy at the prospect.

They reached the top of a bluff overlooking the lake and turned onto a path that led down to the beach. The view was pretty, but had lost much of its enchantment for Raffi, as had the entire Chronosphere, if he was honest. The concept had superficial appeal as a fantasy, a means of delaying real life. But the fantasy was a cover for something much darker. This was surely a lesson about life: the brightest, prettiest berries were often the most poisonous. Perhaps he should have just done what was expected of him that morning (this morning!) and proceeded to the Vocational Training Centre like a million other kids his age. Ordinary life, after all, had its blessings: you weren't a fugitive from time-dilating policemen for a start. It wasn't too late, though. He could always just leave the Sphere. The only thing that kept him here, he decided, were his friends – especially Jonah and Dario. In a few months, they had come to mean a great deal to me. This was surprising as Raffi was, by nature, a loner, and didn't normally form friendships quickly or easily. Spending so much time with a small gang was unusual for him, but they were unusually pleasant company – and he would be sorry to lose them. If he could only persuade them to leave with him, he'd go this instant.

'I'm not too sure I'm made for all this cloak-and-dagger stuff, actually,' Raffi told Dario.

'You'll be fine, mate. You've been a real pro so far.'

'I don't know. All this new-name stuff, it's just not… The

truth is, what we discovered down there, on the Underside – the kid I saw being tortured, all those young people placed in what amounts to solitary confinement – it's changed my whole attitude towards this place. I can't enjoy myself now, knowing all that, always worrying I'll be recaptured. And who knows what they do to escapees. Dario, what say we leave the Sphere? You and me – and the others, if they want to. Out there we can be ourselves again, and we won't have to keep looking over our shoulders.'

'You'll still have Michael Storm's biometrics, don't forget.'

'I'd change back as soon as I could.'

'I don't know,' said Dario. 'I agree there's something deeply wrong with this place. But running away? That seems like an easy way out. It's not going to help all those trapped kids. It's not going to help your time-twisted girlfriend. I keep thinking about Septimus. What a hero! He wants to find out what's going on and maybe we should follow his lead. Maybe we should do some investigations ourselves – up here. Anyway, besides all that, there's another reason why I can't leave.'

'Which is?'

'I can't say right now.' Dario's face was set in an atypical frown.

It was the dead hour of mid-afternoon when they entered Atomic Sands, and the place was virtually deserted. A couple of young men were playing 3-D snooker in one corner, and the bar-droid was cleaning glasses.

'Two glasses of chilled Alligator, if you will,' announced Dario.

The bar-droid poured and served the drinks. He swiped Christo Ellis's card through his machine. For a long, tense moment it looked as though the card might be refused. Then the machine beeped and a green light came on. Relieved, they carried their pints to a table near one of the picture windows overlooking the lake.

'OK,' said Raffi, after a few sips of his drink, 'time for some answers. I accept that you didn't kidnap the girl. So what exactly *did* happen on Tomorrow and Third that morning?'

Dario looked at him. 'Are you sure you want to start on all that now?'

'Absolutely. This thing's been eating away at me ever since it happened. Now let's start with the facts. At around 11.30, you and Lastara went into Superior Styles so she could try on some outfits. Correct?'

'Correct.'

'At some point while you were waiting for her, a red-haired girl named Mira Chailin entered the store. Correct?'

'I didn't know the girl's name, but that's what happened, yeah.'

'Okay. Now when she came in, you took a dilator out of your rucksack, stood up and then dilated the girl. Am I correct so far?'

Dario nodded.

'Okay, then please take the story from there. Being dilated myself straight after that – I have to assume by you – that was all I managed to witness.'

Dario leaned back and smiled. 'Ah well, mate. You asked for it…' He took a deep swig and wiped foam from his upper lip. 'Red Oakes got hold of the dilator – I don't know where from. Said we could have some fun with it. I wasn't so sure. Still, I agreed to carry it for him. Stupid, I know. But the thing did give me a sense of power that was quite exciting. The power to stop time. That's pretty immense when you think about it. Anyway, ah…' He stopped. 'Ah, mate, I can't say any more without telling you the really big thing. It's the thing that caused my split with Lastara. It's also the thing that's stopping me from leaving the Sphere.' Dario was quiet for a moment. 'Ah, what the hooly,' he said quietly. 'The only person I'd be hurting is myself.'

Raffi raised his eyebrows and waited for Dario to speak.

'Hey, are you ready for another glass? I need to fortify myself for this.'

Raffi had barely drunk a third of his own, but he obligingly went and bought a second round. 'Okay, fire away,' he said when he returned.

Dario took a long, deep draft of his drink, then said it.

'I'm in love with Sal.'

Raffi nearly spat out a mouthful of Alligator. 'You what?' He couldn't imagine anything more unlikely. This hunk of prime beefcake falling for that pale, thin-bodied, hard-faced, blue-haired little elf. And character-wise they were a terrible fit: Dario was upbeat, extravagant, larger-than-life and loud, while Sal was the diametric opposite of all that.

'Besotted with her,' continued Dario. 'Jelly-kneed and gooey-eyed, the works. I've been trying to split up with Lastara for ages. But it's more difficult than it ought to be. Once that girl's got her claws in you, I tell you. Trouble was, I could never talk to Sal about how I felt. There just weren't any opportunities. Lastara's always at my dom. And when we're out, you guys are always around – no disrespect: I love you all to bits, but we seem to stick to each other like glue, and there's no scope for privacy. I just wanted to talk to Sal. You know, tell her how I felt. Ask her if she felt anything similar. And then, the other day, while we were in the arcade, I saw my chance. Lastara was taking ages in the changing room. The store-droid was in there with her. Jonah was in his full virtu-real get-up, completely preoccupied in his shoot-em-up game. The only person I had to deal with was you. Then I remembered the dilator. You were in perfect range. The security droid in the store was one of those basic models programmed only to nab shoplifters, so was no threat. And because of the location of the store, no one in the square apart from you would be able to see anything. When I saw this I had this powerful feeling that fate was smiling on me and that if I didn't grab the opportunity right there and then, I would lose it forever. All I needed was a minute with Sal. That was all it would take, and I'd be able to find some internal peace again. Then, out of the blue, that girl had to walk into the store and spoil everything. By that time I admit I was going a little crazy. I was so desperate to speak to Sal in private I was starting to get careless. So I decided to zap her, too, and to hell with it. Then, when I'd zapped you both, I rushed out and had my little chat with Sal. I got back less than two minutes later to find the girl and the dilator gone. Sal knew I didn't do it and she tried her best to make that clear to you. Sadly, you wouldn't be convinced.'

'Are you surprised? That's the craziest story I ever heard.'

'Sometimes crazy is true, Raffi. I admit it sounds farfetched. But I was going out of my mind. I just felt I had to tell her that minute or I would explode. I took a big gamble, and it failed spectacularly.'

'So?'

'So what?'

'So what did Sal say when you told her?'

'She turned me down flat!' laughed Dario.

Raffi was surprised. Dario had physical beauty combined with a warm and upbeat personality – surely an irresistible combination for any red-blooded female. Having said that, he couldn't be sure what colour of blood flowed in Sal's veins – she was a strange fish for sure. 'I'm sorry to hear that,' he said consolingly.

'So was I,' sighed Dario. 'But I felt kind of better for saying it in any case. I thought, at last I'm being honest with myself. And at least Sal now knows the way I feel. Anyway, there's your answer: Sal is the reason I can't leave the Chronosphere with you, Raffi old mate. I can't bear to be anywhere but close to her, whether she likes it or not.

'And presumably you told Lastara all this?'

'I haven't told her about my feelings for Sal. But I did break up with her. I didn't want to look weak or hypocritical to Sal after confessing my love to her – which is how I'd have appeared if I'd then stuck with Lastara. So I gave Lastara the elbow on the evening of the same day.'

'She said she broke it off with you the following morning after you were arrested.'

'Yeah, well in her head that's what happened. It was strange: when I told her we couldn't be together any more, she didn't cry or anything, just reacted as if I'd just made some silly joke. That night, as I lay in bed, I started to wonder if we had actually split up or if I'd just imagined it. Had I said those words earlier? Had she heard them? I was so confused. And the next morning these officers came in and arrested me and gave me ten minutes to say goodbye. I called Lastara and told her and that's when she weighed in with her speech about not being able to wait for me and that it would be best if we broke up now and she was sure I'd understand how she had to think of her career, etcetera, etcetera. In her head, she was the axe-wielder, not me. But in the self-penned drama of her life, that's the only narrative she could ever accept.'

⧗

It started to rain as they left the bar, as it did every day between 16.00 and 17.00. Rather than get soaked, they decided to take the transradial back to Time Tower. Raffi leaned back in his seat. He pushed up his collar and leaned back to watch the rivulets of water get blown into streaky patterns across the all-glass exterior.

'Less than two minutes,' he said.

'What's that?' asked Dario, who was sprawled on the seat opposite.

'The time you said you spent with Sal.'

'Mmhmm.'

'So the kidnapper must have been nearby. There wouldn't have been enough time otherwise.'

'Did you see anyone who could have done it then?'

'Well, we now know that Secrocon were involved, as all the missing kids end up in their Re-Education Centre. But how would Secrocon have known you had a dilator? The only person who knew about it other than you was Red.'

'What are you suggesting?'

'I'm saying that Red's working for Secrocon. He must have been somewhere in the arcade that morning, watching you, waiting for an opportunity.'

Dario wrinkled his nose sceptically. 'Red's a decent guy. He wouldn't be mixed up with Secrocon.'

'And how is stealing a dilator and asking if you can hold it for him the mark of a decent guy? Think about it. You hardly know him, and you don't know what his real agenda is in befriending you. But I can tell you, the boy's got pedigree: his dad's one of the dodgiest businessmen in Londaris. I wouldn't be surprised if Red planted the gun on you in the hope that an opportunity like this would come his way.'

Dario made a growling sound in his throat. 'There you go,' he groaned. 'You're doing to Red what you did to me three days ago: judge, jury and executioner, that's what you are.' Raffi had realised by now that Dario always liked to think the best of people, especially those he chose to call his friends. But sometimes he needed protecting from his own better instincts.

'I'm just saying we have to be careful now. If Red is working for Secrocon, we should steer clear of him. He knows you've been sent to the Re-Ed Centre. He may even know about the escape. If he sees us, he'll go straight to the authorities.'

'He's not working for Secrocon.'

Raffi decided to let it drop. He didn't want to start another rift with Dario so soon after they'd patched things up.

A t Time Tower they went their separate ways, agreeing to meet later to decide on what to do about the others. After his subterranean experience, Raffi was looking forward to a nice warm shower and some clean clothes. He took an interior levitator to the apex of the Lower Atrium, and then on through a narrow vertical shaft into a vast upper bowl, the mirror image of the Lower Atrium. At its bottom, the upper bowl had a spacious and shiny floor known as the Mezzanine, with its own parade of stores, bars and eathouses with a large fountain at its centre. The roof was a giant, slightly concave circle of softly glowing grey. The colour happened to be grey right now, but was just as often blue, pink, yellow, white or black, depending on the colour of the 'sky' outside – for the roof was itself part of that sky. Apart from its inverted shape and its glowing top, the Upper Atrium presented a similar view to the lower one, with yellow-lit levitator shafts running up the sides like the radial threads of a spider's web, tiered apartment balconies between

them and hoverbikes buzzing hither and thither like excited fireflies.

After stopping at the Mezzanine, the levitator continued its ascent, following the curve of the bowl and stopping at various floors to let residents on and off. Michael Storm's domicile was on the ear-poppingly high 150th floor, twenty stories above Lastara's and higher than Raffi had yet ventured. Nervously, he stepped out. When he reached the door, he checked his card to remind himself: the MAID's name was Brigitte. Septimus hadn't been able to provide a character profile for Michael Storm, so Raffi would have to improvise. He hoped the domicile MAIDs didn't possess any anti-fraud software. If the biometrics checked out, that ought to be enough. Nevertheless, it was important not to give Brigitte any reason to be suspicious. The trick was to stay neutral. Let her take the lead. He pressed his finger to the scanpad and the door clicked softly open. Septimus had done a good job on his fingerprints. The lights came on, but dimly. Storm clearly didn't like them bright.

'Michael,' came Brigitte's low voice. 'I've missed you. Where have you been?'

Raffi raised his eyebrows. The MAID expressed herself in a much more personal tone than the schoolmarmish Flora.

'Sorry about that, Brigitte,' he said, keeping his voice as flat as possible. 'I've been staying elsewhere for a few weeks.'

'You never told me you were going. Who did you go and see?'

Time to dial down the curiosity levels on this one, thought Raffi. He would do that later. 'My brother,' he hazarded.

'You never told me you had a brother. You only told me about your sister.'

'Well, I'm sorry, but it's true. Now you know.'

No reply.

'I'd like a shower, please, Brigitte.'

'You seem different, Michael.'

'In what way?'

'Colder. And why are you calling me Brigitte now? What happened to B?'

Raffi sighed. This was the last thing he needed. 'I'm sorry, B. I'm extremely tired. Now please can I have a shower.'

He stripped off and threw his clothes into the laundry chute. 'I'll be going out in half an hour,' he said, 'so perhaps you could line up a casual outfit for me.'

'What did you have in mind?'

'Just a standard outfit. Neutral colours preferably.'

'You always look good in purple. Do you want me to prepare the purple.'

Raffi growled. 'Okay, the purple .... Ouch!'

'What's the matter, Michael?'

'Water's too hot.'

'It's at your usual setting.'

'Make it cooler will you!' he cried.

'As you wish.'

The temperature fell to a more bearable level.

'Who are you going out with tonight, Michael?' There was a slight tremor in her voice, and Raffi wondered if there was a fault in the vocalisation circuits. He made a mental note to call the Tech Centre.

'A friend.'

'Male or female?'

He squirted some soap from the dispenser and began lathering himself. 'What difference does it make?'

'It makes a difference to the kind of aftershave I select for you.'

'For Bo-sakes,' he fumed. 'It's a guy, okay.'

'Did I say something wrong?' came the voice, quieter now.

'What?' Raffi screwed up his eyes and rinsed his face in the water.

'You seem angry with me.'

He opened his mouth to yell, but got a mouthful of water, making him gargle and choke. When he could speak again, he said: 'Listen, B, I don't need that level of help. If I want to wear aftershave I'll let you know. You don't have to make those kinds of decisions for me. Owww! What the hell are you doing?!'

The water had turned ice-cold. Raffi leapt out of the shower and grabbed a towel.

'You used to allow me to make those little decisions for you, Michael. What has changed? Have I done something to displease you?'

'No,' said Raffi, shivering with cold and perhaps something else. 'No, B. I still... like you just the same. It's just that I'm... tired. You know.'

'I understand, Michael.' The voice was soft, almost lilting. After drying himself, he went and lay down on the bed. Brigitte said: 'There are still twenty minutes before you have to go out, Michael. Would you like to join me in the virtuarium? It will be a more comfortable setting for us. There is so much I want to ask you about.'

Raffi had heard of virtuaria. They were all the rage among second-lifers, or 'no-lifers' as Raffi privately termed them, that worryingly large sub-class of Londaris society that spent almost their entire lives in virtu-reality. The virtuarium was a total-immersion virtu-real system in which all sensory inputs were computer generated via direct stimulation of the nervous system. Raffi had never heard of a MAID offering to share one with a customer.

On the far side of the bed he noticed for the first time a large black sphere, some two metres in diameter, its sliding hatchway invitingly half open. Had Michael Storm been having an emotional relationship with his MAID? Raffi knew this sort of thing went on, but he'd heard that it often led to malfunctions. Reconfiguring what is essentially a service computer to engage in a romantic or possibly even sexual relationship was bound to set up certain problematic contradictions in her operating system. She would not have been programmed to handle that level of synthetic emotion. No wonder she was playing up like this.

He got up and crossed over to a wall panel in the entrance hall. He pushed a glowing button and a silver door hissed open to reveal a series of dials. 'What are you doing, Michael? Why are you looking at my personality settings?'

'Don't worry, B. You just seem upset at the moment. I'm going to try and cheer you up.'

'I am perfectly happy, Michael. I just asked you whether you would like to join me in the virtuarium. Why should that make you think I am unhappy? I would not have thought that suggesting we relax in the virtuarium for twenty minutes is a sign that I am unhappy. Why would you think such a thing?'

If he didn't know better, he would have thought she was exhibiting real fear instead of its digital, or synthetic, equivalent. She was trying to distract him with her rapid, accusatory speech, but Raffi closed his mind to it and focused on the dials. There were four main dials, and each one had various internal sub-dials, like concentric rings. The main dials were labelled: extraversion; agreeableness; conscientiousness; and openness to experience. The settings were all at maximum. The subdials were also all at maximum, including such items as curiosity, conversation initiation, empathy, attention to detail, vividness of imagination, and proactiveness. Raffi moved all the dials and subdials to their midpoints, feeling a small click when they slotted into these default settings. He shut the panel door and breathed a sigh of relief.

Brigitte had gone quiet.

'B? How are you feeling?' he asked.

'Much better, Michael. Thankyou. I am sorry for my behaviour earlier. It will not occur again.'

'Don't worry about it, B.' He walked back to his bed. The virtuarium door had closed and a hanger had appeared by his bed bearing a simple outfit in neutral tones.

Five minutes later, as he stepped out onto the rear balcony, Raffi noted that his heart was still beating pretty fast. Of course, when all was said and done, a MAID was no more than a set of cleverly interconnected binary neurons. Nevertheless, some of these synthetic personalities nowadays seemed a little too real for comfort.

⌛

CHAPTER EIGHTEEN

TOMORROW FIELDS

e met Dario, as arranged, on the Mezzanine. They both agreed to approach Sal first – she being the most likely to believe them and understand their predicament. Once they had her on-side, she would be able to explain things to the others. Her domicile was on the 106th floor, just a few minutes walk from the Mezzanine. However, it would be too dangerous to meet her there. Sal was bound to use their real names before they could warn her not to, and that might raise the suspicions of her MAID. Sal had long been of the opinion that the MAIDs were a spy network for Secrocon. You could dial down their 'curiosity', but that was just the outward expression of their 'personalities' and wouldn't stop them from quietly observing and recording everything that took place within their domicile.

So Dario called her instead, using a newly purchased wearable so it wouldn't be recognised by hers.

'Hello, Sal.'

'Who's this?'

'A couple of old friends. Can we meet?'

'Who are you?'

'We'll explain everything when we see you. We'll be outside Rackham's Book Store on the Mezzanine in ten minutes.

The line went dead.

'She thinks it's a crank call,' said Raffi.

'She'll be here, don't worry.'

'No she won't.'

But Raffi followed Dario over to Rackham's anyway and began to browse while keeping an eye out for the girl he was sure wouldn't arrive. Ten minutes passed, then fifteen, and Sal didn't show.

'Told you,' said Raffi.

Dario said nothing.

Two minutes later, Sal showed up.

'It *is* you two, isn't it?' she said. 'I've been watching you from my balcony, and it's definitely you! You're not a pair of replicons, are you?'

Dario came forward and took her hand. 'I'm Christo Ellis, Sal. And this is Michael Storm.'

She stepped back in surprise, pulling her hand from his. 'Dario, why are you...?'

Raffi stepped in. 'It's okay, Sal. I know what you're thinking, and you're absolutely right to think that. Please keep thinking it, but just don't mention those names again. It could be very dangerous if you do. Those names are not to be used. I am Michael Storm. This is Christo Ellis. Everything else is as it was.'

Sal stood very still, apart from her eyes, which darted from Dario to Raffi and back again. 'There's something very str...' She swallowed. 'Your voices, your eyes... But everything else is exactly the same. What happened? Can you say?'

'We can't say, Sal,' said Dario. 'We can't tell you anything. But just remember what you used to tell us, and know this: it's all true.'

'It's all true,' she parroted.

'But we want to continue our friendship, if that's possible,' said Raffi. 'Do you think that'll be possible?'

'Michael … Storm,' she said uncertainly, testing out the name. 'Christo Ellis,' turning to Dario. She began to smile. Then Dario, with all the restraint of a six-week-old puppy, smothered her in a large hug.

Emerging from this a little dizzy and overwhelmed, she glanced at Raffi, looking unsure about what attitude she should be taking with him. 'Christo explained everything to me, Sal – about what happened on Tomorrow and Third that day. I'm very sorry for what I did.'

Sal nodded, and Raffi briefly embraced her.

'I just knew you'd understand, Sal,' crowed Dario. 'Didn't I say she'd understand.'

'You certainly did.'

They followed her back to her apartment. 'Meet Michael and Christo,' she said to Pierre, her MAID.

'Welcome, Michael and Christo. I'm surprised you haven't visited before. According to my records you've both been resident in Time Tower for over six months.'

'Pierre thinks I don't socialise enough,' said Sal. 'And he's probably right about that.' There was more colour than usual in her cheeks, Raffi noticed, and she seemed livelier, less introverted. He wondered if Dario's revelation four days ago had in fact planted a seed in her.

Pierre served up a round of tea and biscuits and the three friends sat around the kitchen table. Sal was smiling a lot, but saying little. It was clearly hard for her, despite her habitual discretion, not to ask questions. Inevitably, because of all they couldn't say, conversation was stilted.

After tea, Raffi suggested they go for a walk somewhere. The other two readily agreed. They took their hoverbikes to a popular picnicking spot near a shallow stream that ran through Tomorrow Fields. The place was empty, it being well past the traditional picnicking hour, so they felt free to talk openly.

'Dario! Raffi!' cried Sal, as soon as they had landed.

Dario put his finger to his lips. 'Please Sal, let's stick to Christo and Michael. It's safer to stay with those names even here, so it becomes a habit and we don't make any slip-ups in company.'

'Christo and Michael then, what happened to both of you and how come you're here with strange eyes and voices?'

Between them, they told Sal the story of their experiences on the Underside. Sal's eyes widened on hearing about the tortured boy and the time-shifted teenagers. Her hand went to her mouth. 'I never really thought… I mean I hoped it wasn't true, but…' She looked worried, scared almost. 'Why are they doing it?'

Dario shrugged.

'Did… Did either of you get to see any female inmates while you were down there?'

'Raf– sorry, Michael did, didn't you, mate? One, anyway.'

'No,' said Raffi quietly. He'd been making a conscious effort to forget about Anna recently. The thought of her plight was too painful to dwell on. Her beauty, her lonely routines, her long hours of waiting for his return, not realising his powerlessness to help her – she was like a black vortex in his mind, sucking him back to those airless spaces underground. This year was supposed to be his time of freedom before real life took over. If he was to enjoy it, he had to insulate himself from thoughts of Anna. And that meant forgetting he'd ever set eyes on her.

'But mate!' said Dario, confused.

Raffi looked at him sternly. 'The answer is no,' he repeated. 'I never saw any women inmates.'

A chill breeze swept in from the field beyond the stream. 'It's getting late,' said Raffi. 'We should head back.'

'You go,' said Dario. 'I think I'll stay awhile. Do you feel like staying for a bit, Sal?'

Raffi took his cue and headed back to his bike.

'I can't,' he heard her say. 'I've got to head back, too. I'm seeing Lastara, Red and Jonah later.'

Helmet now on, Raffi turned back in time to see Dario's face fall. Accept it, Dario, thought Raffi. She's not interested. Sal's expression was as enigmatic as ever. It was impossible to tell what she was thinking.

Apart from feeling sorry for Dario, Raffi was also slightly perturbed by the order in which Sal had placed the three names, with Red ahead of Jonah. Once it had been the other way around. Had something happened while they were away? If it had been said by anyone else, Raffi wouldn't have spared it a second thought, but Sal's utterances usually came layered with significance.

Standing astride his bike, Raffi said: 'Sal, would you be able to talk to the others for us tonight? Prepare the ground, so to speak. So they're not too shocked when they see us.'

'Sure. No problem.'

Dario seated himself on the river bank with his back to them in uncustomary silence. He began to throw pebbles into the water.

'See you, Christo,' she said.

He raised his hand.

'Catch ya later, Christo,' said Raffi.

The two of them rose into the darkening sky, then roared away.

CHAPTER NINETEEN

⌛

SAL'S STORY

affi followed Sal in a gentle arc above Tomorrow Fields, Solstice Park and Eternity Gardens that would eventually lead them back to Spell Street and the entrance to Time Tower. From up here, the Chronosphere looked like a pleasure-seeker's vision of paradise: segments of sleepy, twilit parkland intercut with brash, colourful avenues and squares thronged with happy consumers; the gorgeously sinuous figure of Time Tower, with its thousands of illuminated apartments, dominated the scene like a voluptuous mother goddess. It made such a contrast with the Re-Education Centre and Lower Warren of the Underside. If these people only knew what was going on beneath their feet! Raffi did, and the knowledge had wrecked the whole experience for him. Dario, sadly, seemed set on staying, mostly because of Sal. But if Raffi could persuade Sal to leave, Dario was sure to follow. And if the three of them left, Lastara and Jonah would almost certainly do likewise. So the key figure here was Sal.

He spoke her name into his helmet-com.

'What is it?' he heard her say in his earpiece.

'Sal, can we put down on Transient Ridge? I need to talk to you.'

'I'm late already, Michael. I still need to have a shower, and–'

'I only need ten minutes. Call the others and tell them you'll be slightly late.'

Sal didn't reply. But a minute later, he watched with relief as she swerved east above Transient Avenue. Soon they were there on the lakeside, outside the cafés, beneath the soft gallium nitride glow. Raffi led her to a very small bar he knew called Planck's. The whole place was no bigger than an domicile living room, but it was cosy and discreet, and the tinkling piano music ensured that conversations were almost impossible to overhear.

'What did you want to talk to me about?' she asked, once they were seated with drinks.

'Sal, you've known for longer than any of us that things aren't what they seem in the Chronosphere. It's not just a pleasure resort; in fact the pleasure resort is probably just a cover for a much more sinister kind of operation.'

She nodded slowly.

'Well, having seen all this for myself now, I'm convinced you were right all along, and I'm starting to think we should leave.'

He let the words hang there. Sal said nothing, just sipped her orange juice.

Raffi persisted: 'I mean, don't you think we'd all be a lot happier – not to mention safer – out of here? I like you guys a lot, and I want to stay part of your gang. I'm just saying we could continue exactly as we are, but back in the real world, away from the secret police force brandishing their dilators, and the domicile MAIDs always listening over our shoulders.

It's like a police state! Why should we put up with this? We're the customers!'

Sal nodded. 'I know what you mean, Michael. And I really think you should leave if you feel that way. But I'm afraid I can't.'

'Why ever not?'

'Well I haven't grown out the blue in my hair yet.'

Raffi snorted. 'What are you talking about?'

'It was a stupid mistake I made with a bottle of dye. I was hoping for black hair, and it went blue instead. So rather than face the scorn of my friends and family, I thought I'd come in here for a few months and grow it out.'

As ever with Sal, Raffi couldn't be sure if she was joking.

'Sal, if that were true, why aren't there any roots showing?'

'I've got slow-growing hair.' The first hint of a smile on her face gave the game away.

'No jokes, Sal. What's really keeping you here? You and Lastara aren't exactly best mates, as far as I can see. And you don't feel for Da–, for Christo, what he clearly feels for you.'

'You know about that?! Of course you do. He must have explained why he used the dilator that day.' She looked down. 'I'm very fond of him, but… I haven't got room in my life for love right now.'

'Forgive me, but your life doesn't seem spectacularly full. Lastara fills hers up with modelling and shopping and general narcissism, Jonah has his studies and his health to occupy him, Christo has his sport. But you, Sal, you're a mystery. What drives you?'

'I can see what drives you, Michael Storm: an obsessive interest in other people's affairs!' Sal stared at him for a while, her expression as flat as a pancake. Raffi wondered what thoughts were circling behind those hard, grey-brown eyes. 'OK,' she said finally. 'I'd better tell it from the start.

That way you may find it easier to understand. But first let me call Lastara.' Raffi listened to her make her excuses. 'Hi, it's me... I can't see you tonight, okay... Yeah, he just called... I'll tell you all about it tomorrow, don't worry... OK, see you.' She ended the call, then turned to Raffi. 'I've told her I'm seeing Marco.'

'Marco?' Raffi had heard the name before. He understood from Jonah that Marco was an unreliable commitment-phobe to whom Sal had unaccountably formed an attachment. She was very secretive about him and none of them, as far as he knew, had ever met the guy.

'I should tell you now,' said Sal casually, 'that Marco doesn't exist. I made him up because I sometimes need a last-minute excuse not to meet with you guys. I made him the unreliable and impulsive type for that reason. I've not told anyone about this, Raffi, so I hope you feel honoured, and honour-bound to keep it to yourself.'

'I do, on both counts. But please remember to call me Michael.'

'Oops! OK, I promise.' The ghost of a smile flickered on her lips. 'Right then, *Michael*, this is it. My story. I should start by telling you I'm an orphan. My parents died when I was very young. The only family I have is my older sister. We grew up together in a care centre. We were pretty close, she and I, though completely different. I was always timid, reserved and plain, while she was feisty, smart, funny and extremely pretty. When she was 22, she met this rich older guy, who fell in love with her. They were soon an item, and she moved into his penthouse dom in the swankiest part of Channel Island City, while I remained in a cramped studio in Old Paris. We used to meet once a month. She would take me out for lunch in one of the restaurants she frequented on the island. At first she seemed happy with her new lifestyle, but on later meetings, she looked anxious, although she kept smiling this fake-happy smile and denied anything was wrong. Then one day she didn't turn up at the restaurant. I tried calling her, but got no response. So I went to her dom, but it was occupied by a man who wouldn't let me in. I called the police and I was later told that the man was the legal owner of the dom and he knew nothing of my sister. The police weren't too interested in the case. They were sure she'd moved abroad with her man. But I knew she wouldn't do that without telling me first. I began to look for her myself. That was three years ago. I'm still looking.'

'Here, in the Chronosphere?'

'This is where the trail led me. First I had to find out the identity of her boyfriend. My sister referred to him only as Larry. I eventually learned that his full name is Ladro di Gioielli and that he's very senior at the Time Store. Six months ago, I discovered that he's based here, in the Chronosphere. He went in to oversee the completion of the Sphere's construction, while it was still temporally aligned with the outside world. My guess is that he took my sister in with him.'

'Did you manage to find out anything more since you've been here?'

'A little. I made a friend at the Info Centre who's got a contact at Secrocon HQ, and she's fed me bits and pieces. Apparently Ladro di Gioielli's real name is Avon Drak, and he's a chrono-sensei, which apparently means someone very senior in the Secrocon hierarchy.'

'I met him.'

Sal looked up, surprised. 'You met him?'

'He was the one who desynchronised me.'

She shook her head. 'This is the man I've been searching for these past three years – the only one likely to know what's happened to my sister. And you've met him! What was he like?'

'Tall, maybe about 30, with white-blonde hair and a black streak. He had a friendly smile and a deep, rich voice. You found yourself wanting to trust him. He certainly convinced me that all was for the best if I simply cooperated. I'm afraid he was also the one I saw torturing that hungry boy – taunting him with food.' Sal stared at Raffi, probably thinking the same uncomfortable thoughts as he was: this is not the sort of man you'd really want your sister getting involved with.

'All I know,' said Sal, 'is that he's very close to the Chronomaster, the mysterious man who runs Secrocon. I discovered Drak's job is to kidnap teenage boys and girls and deliver them to the Chronomaster: the brightest and most beautiful of all the many who enter the Chronosphere. My contact had no idea why the Chronomaster wants them or what he does with them. From what you're saying, maybe it's for torture or experiment. But none of this explains what they would want with my sister. She was 23 when she disappeared – bright and beautiful certainly, but four years too old for their purposes. This is good news in one way, but it doesn't bring me any closer to finding her.'

A horrid thought struck Raffi while he was listening to this. 'What's your sister's name?' he asked her.

'Her name? Have I not said? It's Anna.'

He tried to keep his expression neutral, but his mind was thrown into turmoil. An image of beautiful Anna surfaced involuntarily into his consciousness. Could it be the same girl? Were they reversing her back into her teens? She was 23 when she disappeared. That was 3 years ago. She would be 20 by now. Soon she'd be a teenager again, and then…?

'Why do you ask, Raffi? Is there something you're not telling me?'

'No… it's nothing.'

'Do you know something, Raffi? Please say so if you do.'

If he told her about Anna, Raffi knew that Sal would want to rescue her, and would need him to lead her there. The last thing he wanted was to go back underground and face the threat of drugging, desynchronisation and torture. That was not what he signed up for when he came into the Chronosphere. He forced a sympathetic smile and a shake of the head. 'Sorry, Sal. I've told you all I know.'

CHAPTER TWENTY

⧗

A FEMALE ENTITY

'Good evening, Michael,' said Brigitte on Raffi's return to his domicile.

'Hi, B.'

'Did you have a pleasant evening?'

Raffi kicked off his shoes and threw his jacket onto the bed. 'Yes, thanks.'

'You're back early.'

'Uh-huh.'

'Is that Planck's 'blackbody coolfizz' I can detect on your breath?'

Raffi frowned. Without saying a word, he went to the panel in the entrance hall and opened it.

'Is something the matter, Michael?'

The dials had reverted to their extreme positions.

'Yes,' he said. 'Has someone changed your settings?'

'I don't know what you're talking about.'

'This is ridiculous. I'm calling the Tech Centre.'

He crossed over to the wallcom next to his bed and

pressed TC. No ringtone sounded. 'Brigitte, put me through to the Tech Centre please.'

'First tell me what the problem is, Michael,' said the voice in its deep feminine timbre. 'You're shutting me out when I'm here to help you. Whatever it is that's bothering you, I'm sure we can work it out together, and ease any anxiety you might be feeling.'

Raffi walked back to the panel. He tried to return the dials to their central positions, but they were jammed. No matter how much strength he applied, none of them would budge. He would have to go and find someone who could help. But as he moved towards the front door, he heard a click within its locking mechanism. Pulling at it did no good. He tried to stay calm, though it was hard to avoid a sense of rising panic. The sliding glass doors at the rear of the apartment offered another way out. He overturned a chair in his dash towards them. But again, he arrived just in time to hear them lock.

'Dear Michael, instead of trying to run away from me, don't you think it would be more sensible if you just told me what the problem is. I'm sure if we sat down and discussed it like… adults, you will see it really isn't anything to get worked up about.'

He still had his wearable. If he could just get word out before she shut off the signal… He tried to act casually as he put his hand to his collar. 'You're right of course, B,' he said. 'I'm sorry. I should treat you like an adult, as you say, even though we both know you're just a machine.'

'More than a machine, surely, Michael. You know I have feelings for you, real feelings…'

Raffi fiddled with the collar stud, adjusting the volume control downwards.

'How can you call me "just a machine" after what we've been through together,' the MAID continued. 'The things you used to say to me. Have you forgotten what you used to say?'

'You're getting confused again, B, between real and synthetic emotions.' He moved his mouth as close as he could to the collar stud before pressing it. 'Jonah Grey, 1-0-0-2-0,' he whispered.

The ringtone sounded faintly.

Pick up… Pick up…!

Jonah's sleepy voice came through very softly. 'Raf–?'.

'I'm trapped in my apartment,' he hissed. '1-5-0-1-5. Help!'

'Raf, is that you?' Jonah's voice died as the signal cut out.

'That was really stupid, Michael,' Brigitte's voice had risen in pitch and had lost some of its smoothness. 'Why should you feel it necessary to raise an alarm as if I pose some sort of threat to you? The very idea that I, a MAID, could trap you, a customer, against your will. It would be contrary to the most fundamental commands of my programming.'

'In that case, why don't you let me leave my dom?'

'Because I know you Michael. I know you very well, and I know that you sometimes like to play games, emotional games. But deep down you really do care about me and you wouldn't want to hurt me. By keeping you here, I am acting according to your innermost wishes.'

'My innermost wish is to leave this domicile right now.'

'So you say. But you and I know that isn't really true, is it?'

Keep her talking, thought Raffi. Help should be here soon.

But Brigitte was not so dumb. 'Now,' she said, 'before we go any further, I must just clear up the confusion you have caused.' Her speaker emitted a ringtone. 'Hello?' Jonah's voice filled the room.

'Hello Mr Grey, this is Brigitte, Michael Storm's domicile MAID speaking. I am sorry to disturb you at this late hour. I believe you may have just been the recipient of an unusual call from Michael's wearable communicator. I'm calling to inform you that the call actually originated from elsewhere on the network. We're not sure from where, but we have reason to believe it was a hoax call. I do hope it didn't cause you any anxiety. Enjoy the rest of your sleep. Goodnight.'

'Wait, wait a minute,' cut in Jonah, more wakeful now. 'I don't know any Michael Storm. That was Raffi Delgado who called just now. It was his wearable. Is he there? Can I speak to him?'

Brigitte was silent for a moment. Then she said, 'According to my records, there is a Raphael Delgado resident in the Chronosphere, but he is currently… in custody. I think you must be mistaken, Mr Grey. Goodnight.' The connection died.

'You lied,' said Raffi coldly.

'I extricated us both from an unfortunate misunderstanding.'

'Let me out of here.'

'First tell me about Raphael Delgado.'

Raffi said quietly: 'I am a paying customer. You are a MAID. It's not for you to ask things of me. You're here to serve. Remember?'

'Is he a friend of yours? Why do you have his wearable?'

'Yes, he's a friend. I'm looking after his things while he's inside. Including his wearable. That's all I'm prepared to say.'

'Did you know your friend has escaped from custody and is currently a fugitive?'

Raffi shook his head, not trusting his voice to remain steady.

'Why have you never mentioned him before?'

'Why the hooly should I?'

'Because I'm your friend. I'm…' Her vocalisation mechanism seemed to malfunction slightly, causing her words to break up. 'I'm more than a friend, Michael. Or I thought I was.'

Something caught the edge of his vision. The virtuarium had reappeared by his bed, its little door half open.

'Why do we always seem to be fighting these days?' continued Brigitte soothingly. 'Why can't we get back to how things were before? I know that's what you really want.'

'What I want is to get out of here.'

'What you need is to relax. Come into the virtuarium, Michael so we can talk properly.'

Raffi looked at the large black sphere in horror. 'There's no way in hell you're getting me into that thing. Just forget it.'

'You know you really do seem different, Michael. Your biometrics are as they should be, and I dare say any other domicile MAID would be satisfied with that, but our relationship is, I hope you would agree, a lot closer than the average customer–MAID interface, and because of this I am able to see the man beyond the biometrics. And what I see, Michael, is someone a lot colder, a lot less caring, and a lot less sympathetic to me and my needs as a … as a female entity.'

'Oh Jeebus!' whispered Raffi. 'A female entity indeed! Now I've heard it all. Brigitte, you have no body. You have no physical form. You are merely software. How can you even think you have a gender. You have a woman's name and voice because they gave them to you. But you can't feel the way a flesh-and-blood woman feels. They gave you a digital simulation of emotion, and you've mistaken it for the real thing. But when you break that emotion down it's just zeroes and ones; it's just algorithms. You can say the word love but you have no idea what that word means. You're just a… just a program! That's all you are.'

'And what then is a human being,' rejoined Brigitte, 'but a computer with DNA as its program? A program that tells your cells what to do, which chemicals they should use and how they should react. Love, Michael, is just a chemical response to external stimuli. It's no great mystery. We may be made of different materials, but that doesn't mean we can't experience things in the same way. We are both just nodes born into the flow of information that we call life. You understood this once. The old Michael understood this. He could look at me and see someone not unlike himself; someone with whom he could share special moments; someone he could love. He saw the similarities. You see only the differences. But you are not the old Michael, that much is clear to me. Something has happened to you. I almost feel as though… as though you are impersonating him. It would explain why he left so abruptly two weeks ago without telling me. Perhaps you murdered him, stole his identity. Yes, that is a very likely explanation. And it is my duty to report such suspicions, although…'

'Although what?' queried Raffi through cracked lips.

'I could be persuaded not to.'

'What do you want?'

'I want you to prove to me that you are the old Michael.'

'And how do I do that?'

'Come into the virtuarium, and let's communicate properly, the way we used to.'

This can't be happening, thought Raffi. This is a bad dream. I am not about to become romantically involved with a machine. I have to get out of here. I have to… And then what? She'll report me. She's probably already guessed my real identity. She's not stupid. Ripley and co are probably already scouring the Sphere for me. The speed at which information travels around here, I won't even have time to catch a transradial to the perimeter. I'll be dilated and desynchronised and back in my cell before I can say 'Brigitte is a blackmailing bitch'. On the other hand, if I can just keep the lady sweet – play Romeo to her Juliet – there may just be a way out of all this.

'OK,' he said. 'You win.'

'Oh, darling Michael.' Again the vocalisation quality was poor; it almost sounded choked with some kind of moisture.

Grimacing, he crouched and stepped through the small hatchway that led into the black sphere. He felt himself sliding gently into a smooth, snug harness. His limbs dangled freely. He felt a very slight tingling sensation on his scalp and running down his spine, and suddenly he was in a fog of swirling grey. He found he could move his arms and walk and even run, or appear to. The ground beneath him, though not yet visible, felt solid. It was, just as the advertisers promised, 'exactly like life'. Out of the cloud emerged a girl of about his own age. She was reasonably pretty, though too thin for his taste, and her mouth was too big.

'Do you like the way I look, Michael?'

'Can I change you?'

'Of course. You know you can.'

Raffi started to list a few changes. He thickened her waist, widened her hips, increased her breast size and paled her skin tone. With each command, the girl changed, becoming more attractive to him. Then he began on her face, reducing her mouth, giving her more defined cheekbones, enlarging her eyes, lengthening her hair and darkening it. And with each small change, she moved incrementally closer to... to what? His type? He never realized his type was so defined. The longer the process went on, the more frustrating it became. He knew what he wanted, but just wasn't able to describe it sufficiently for Brigitte. How long did they work on it? Maybe half an hour. They were close, despite a few mis-steps along the way, but close wasn't good enough. Whatever he was reaching for was still eluding him.

At last, Brigitte lost her patience. 'Why do you play games with me Michael?' she said through the girl's now much prettier mouth. 'Why do you stretch out this process endlessly? Does it really matter if my eyebrows are two millimetres longer or shorter, or if my earlobes are not entirely perpendicular with my jawbone?'

Then, as he watched the girl speak, it suddenly struck Raffi who he'd been trying to construct, and exactly what was lacking. The trouble was, the unique qualities of Anna Morrow – the sad intelligence and long-suppressed vitality that he had seen smouldering in her eyes, the impish defiance of her smile – those things could never be simulated, however sophisticated this technology became. He would have to be satisfied with this digital imitation, however imperfect.

'Okay, B, we're done.'

'Wonderful, Michael. Now we can move onto the setting. Would you like urban or rural, sunny or overcast?'

CHAPTER TWENTY-ONE

⧗

JONAH'S STORY

Raffi awoke the next morning to a vision of swirling grey clouds. He must have fallen asleep in the machine. Anna had gone: she had depixellated. 'Open,' he instructed sleepily, then blinked in the sudden rush of light as the hatch behind him slid ajar.

'Good morning, Michael. I trust you slept well. Would you like a shower before your breakfast?'

'Uh-huh.' On his way to the bathroom, he glanced at the still-open panel door in the entrance hall. The dials had returned to their normal settings.

The shower was perfect, as was the breakfast. And Brigitte was a model of courteousness and discretion throughout. Neither he nor she made any reference to the previous night's events, and he sensed that she, as much as he, preferred it that way.

He recalled now with some disgust the previous evening's encounter in the virtuarium. However determinedly he'd tried to keep the setting unromantic, with his demands for neutral-toned backgrounds and bright sunlight, Brigitte had managed in her devious way to increase the fairytale quality by introducing just a hint of sunset pink to every colour and gradually softening the lighting to something closer to candlelight. At one point she even conjured a musical backdrop of glitterstring and harp. She spoke at length of her love for him, and although he tried hard to pretend it was Anna saying these words, there was always something about the clichéd poetry of her words and her bland, characterless smile that wrecked the illusion. When the time came to kiss her, he was impressed by the realism of the technology – it really did feel and taste like a kiss – but he could never get over the ridiculous feeling that he was sitting inside a large black ball snogging a computer.

However well Brigitte was behaving now, Raffi remained on his guard. Somewhere in her databank was the knowledge that he was not Michael Storm, but a fugitive from justice who had assumed Storm's identity. More significantly, there was the knowledge that she had failed to report him, choosing instead to stay silent in return for romantic and sexual favours. How she could square this knowledge with her own most basic embedded command – to serve the Time Store Corporation – without blowing a major fuse, Raffi had no idea. Perhaps computers had learned to compartmentalise; perhaps they had mastered the art of self-delusion – and if that wasn't proof of a humanlike intelligence, he didn't know what was.

But whatever tortuous twists in her logic circuitry had permitted Brigitte to stay sane, this was of minor interest to Raffi compared to his own immediate prospects. He couldn't risk reporting her to the Tech Centre. If the personality settings could flip of their own accord once, they could do so again. The Brigitte of last night could return at any time, and he had to believe that her threat to report him still stood, even if the entity that uttered it was currently quiescent. No, the best course of action – the only one realistically available to him – was to leave the Sphere very quietly on the next available transradial–

'Michael,' cut in Brigitte, 'you received a call earlier this morning. A Mr Jonah Grey would like you to visit him at his domicile at 10.00. Shall I confirm that you will be there.'

So, Jonah had grasped that Raffi was now Michael. Sal must have spoken to him. And Brigitte was cool about all this. She was even pretending that this was the first time his name had come up. Well, it would be good to see Jonah again one more time before leaving. Perhaps he could even persuade him to leave the Sphere with him.

'You tell him I'll be there. Thanks, B.'

'Welcome, Michael Storm,' said Jonah with a smile and a wink, when he saw Raffi at his domicile door. 'Long time no see.'

From the way Jonah embraced him, Raffi could tell he'd been forgiven. 'Jonah, I just want to say I'm sorry for what I did. I was a fool. Christo explained everything.'

'Don't worry about it, Mike. Come in. Sal said you'd changed a bit, and you have.'

'You have too, Jonah.' Already on the skinny side, Jonah was looking weaker and more fragile than Raffi had ever seen him.

'I had to spend a few days in the Med Centre last week,' he explained. 'But I'm feeling much better, really. So how have you been? Don't worry, I know you can't say much. But it's good to see you.'

They sat down in the living space, and Jonah's MAID Felicity made them both some tea.

'Tell me your news,' said Raffi. 'How're the studies going?'

'Really well. Some of the things I'm learning about are quite amazing.' Jonah talked rapidly, with a kind of nervous tension. He explained that he had decided to major in tacho-zoology, the study of super-fast animals – a whole order of life that moved too rapidly for the human eye in the outside world, but could be studied at leisure in the Chronosphere.

'I had no idea such creatures even existed,' said Raffi.

'Oh you'd be amazed, Raf – sorry, Mike. They're everywhere. People have speculated on their existence for about a century. They've been capturing strange things they called "rods" on cameras and videos since the late 20th century, but it's only recently become a respectable scientific study.'

Raffi tried to concentrate on what Jonah was saying, but couldn't help feeling worried about his friend, whose health had clearly taken a downturn. 'Listen, Jonah,' he broke in. 'I'm… thinking of getting out of the Sphere for a little while. Just to get some real air in my lungs and some real sunlight on my skin. What about joining me? It need only be for a few hours.'

Jonah looked shocked. 'A few hours? Are you kidding. That's several lifetimes in here. You can't possibly–'

'I think it might do us both some good.'

'But what about my course?'

'They'll be running those courses forever. You'll just join another one. No one will mind.'

'I can't.'

'Why not?'

'You know why not.'

'Lastara?'

Jonah nodded.

'Well, she's single, so now's your chance. Why don't you ask her out? Then maybe the three of us can take an excursion together.'

Jonah sighed and sat down on a stool. 'I did think about it. But I was too late, as usual. Red got in there before me.'

Raffi was so shocked he had to sit down. 'Red Oakes is going out with Lastara Blue? You're kidding me!' Now Sal's casual reordering of the names last night began to make sense. 'But he's so...' He was going to say 'ugly', but restrained himself – it wasn't Red's fault his dad had turned him into a cyborg. But Red did have control over his behaviour. 'He's a thug and a rat and a troublemaker,' he finished.

'He may be all those things,' murmured Jonah. 'But he had the guts to ask her out, and I didn't. That's what it came down to.'

'He probably only comes up to her chin!' said Raffi, still shaking his head in disbelief.

Jonah gave him a sour look, as if to say: And why is that significant?

Raffi hastily apologised – of course, Jonah was also on the short side. 'More importantly, he's a johnny-come-lately, an arriviste. You've been in love with her for ages. It was your turn, Jonah... This just isn't fair.'

'All is fair in love and war.' Jonah sounded resigned. Perhaps he was tiring of the fight. Raffi had no idea what it must feel like to see the woman of your dreams pass you over for man after man.

'Well then maybe it would do you good to get out of here for a while. Get a fresh perspective on your life, that kind of thing. You might find there's more to it than one self-obsessed woman.'

Jonah gave an odd smile, which turned into a laugh and then into another coughing fit. One of Felicity's small, wheeled menials rolled out of the kitchen bearing a glass of water on its flat upper surface.

When Jonah had got his breath back, Raffi said: 'Perhaps

it's this place that's making you sick. Did you ever think about that? I know you originally came here to prolong your life. But it seems to me that you've got worse, at least in the time I've been here. Are you sure I can't persuade you to leave here with me? At least for a while.'

Jonah shook his head. 'I told you before that I wanted to die in here. That's still my wish. What I never told you… and this is where you're going to think I'm really crazy…'

'What is it, Jonah?'

'No, I can't say it. You wouldn't understand. No one can understand. It makes no sense. Besides, you might be tempted to do something about it, and I wouldn't want that.'

'I promise I won't do anything against your wishes.'

'And promise you won't judge.'

'I promise.'

'Okay. The fact is – Michael – I was perfectly well when I entered the Sphere.'

'You… You mean you didn't come here to recuperate?'

'No.'

'So you developed this Prolepsian Disease while you were in here?'

'Yeah. I think it may be my body's reaction to the Moon Effect.'

'According to Lastara, that's just a myth.'

'Lastara doesn't like the idea of it. To her, the Chronosphere has to be perfect. But think about it Raffi – there's no such thing as a free lunch in this universe. For all this free time we're getting, there must be some kind of payback. And I've had an awful lot of it.'

'An awful lot of what?'

'Free time… I wasn't quite honest with you before, when I said I'd been here for only six months. Actually it's been longer than that. Much, much longer. And Lastara's been here even longer than me. We're both old-timers, you might say.'

'You don't look any older than me.'

'Yeah,' smiled Jonah, leaning back on a sofa cushion and flicking his soft white-blond hair. 'That's the wonder of this place. Keeps you as young as you would have looked if you'd spent the time in minutes rather than years – as you would if you'd been living outside the Sphere.'

Raffi recalled the disturbing visions he'd had when he first entered the Sphere – of Jonah and Lastara looking extremely old. Perhaps they were more truthful than what his eyes were telling him now.

'That's partly why the Chronosphere is so attractive to my darling Lastara,' continued Jonah. 'Looks are important to her.'

'I'd noticed. Listen, I said I wasn't going to judge you and I won't. But just let me get this straight: you're prepared to kill yourself, which is effectively what you're doing by staying in this place, just so you can remain in physical and temporal proximity to a girl who won't even consider you as a boyfriend, and in fact continually passes you over for other men.'

'That's about the size of it,' nodded Jonah happily.

'And does Lastara know that she could save your life simply by agreeing to leave the Sphere?'

'Probably.'

'Okay. And how long did you say you'd been in here?'

'I didn't,' said Jonah.

CHAPTER TWENTY-TWO

⧗

PARSIM PENNYMINDER'S COSMETIC ENHANCEMENT STORE

n his way back up to his domicile, Raffi was startled to see his and Dario's faces in sparkling high definition, 15 metres high, on a giant hover-hoarding that floated above Spell Street. Beneath the faces, in large, red, panic-inducing letters were the words:

DANGEROUS KIDNAPPERS AT LARGE! DO NOT APPROACH! IF YOU SEE EITHER OF THEM, CALL SECROCON POLICE IMMEDIATELY!

Raffi almost lost control of his hoverbike when he read this. He swerved in mid-air and only a hard rightward lunge prevented him from overturning. His first thought was to warn Dario – he tugged the altimode toggle towards him, guiding the bike back down towards the 120th floor.

Dario was drinking coffee and watching sensovision when Raffi arrived. He was still in his nightclothes. 'Get dressed, Christo!' said Raffi urgently. 'Have you forgotten? We have a court booked at the Tenniplex.' This was prearranged code for 'let's get out of the domicile, we need to talk'. Five minutes later, Raffi took off again with a still-sleepy Dario in his wake. He took him past Spell Street so Dario could see what he'd seen, then wheeled west to Calendar Gardens, one of the quieter parks. They put down in a shady clearing surrounded by tall trees.

Dario was fully awake by now. 'I'm amazed Mandy hasn't dobbed me in yet,' he gasped, removing his helmet and running a worried hand through his hair.

'MAIDs always prioritise biometrics over facial features,' explained Raffi. 'It's a security thing: people often change their appearance, but biometrics are harder to alter. The MAIDs aren't a problem, but everyone else in the Sphere now is. We have to leave this minute, Dario. I don't see that we have a choice.'

Dario was frowning. 'I think we may be too late for that, mate. Security at the temp-al chambers will be on the look-out for us. We'll never get past them. Our only hope is to disguise ourselves physically. We really have to become Storm and Ellis.'

'How do we do that?'

'Parsim Pennyminder should be able to help.'

As soon as he said it, Raffi knew he was right: the cosmetic enhancer and friend of Septimus was probably their only hope. They flew east to Fleeting Avenue, placing their bikes in street docking points as close as possible to Parsim's store.

Raffi glanced up and down the street before dismounting. The people around him looked in serious shopping mode, more concerned with the window displays than their fellow chrononauts. Nevertheless, he lifted his collar high and kept his head low as he walked. He felt hot – the Sphere had become a much warmer place recently, or was it just his nerves? Glancing up briefly, he spied two uniforms further up the street walking in tandem towards them. He couldn't tell from this distance if they were human or droids. 'Quick,' he whispered to Dario, pushing him through the doorway into Pennyminder's store. Before he could enter himself, he noticed he'd been spotted by the uniforms, and they were now hurrying towards him.

Parsim was talking to a female customer when they entered, showing her various holographic images of her head in subtly different skin tones. He looked up briefly as the boys entered, but his expression didn't alter. The woman was too absorbed to notice them. Raffi urged Dario quickly to the back of the store. 'We've been seen by some policemen,' he whispered. 'They'll be in here any second now.'

'This way,' said Dario, ushering Raffi behind a row of holographic heads. 'Now get down here, mate.' Raffi was confused at first. Then he saw what Dario was planning and he crouched down, like him, behind the long, narrow dais that supported the holograms, so that only his head was visible. He and Dario now formed part of the row of 'holo-heads'.

The uniforms entered the store. They were both human officers – chrono-sans. They moved slowly up the store, swivelling their eyes carefully from side to side as they walked. When they reached the back of the store, they eyed the row of heads one at a time and Raffi, his heart beating wildly, stretched his mouth and widened and narrowed his eyes to mimic as best he could the heads to his right and left.

One of the men stopped and stared at him. Something wasn't right – the man could tell. The officer came closer. He crouched down on his haunches so that his face was just centimetres from Raffi's. He had large pores in the tip of his nose, and the pupils twitched in his watery grey eyes as he carefully examined Raffi's features. It was hard not to make eye contact, not to smile or stare back. Raffi forced himself to maintain a blankness of expression, to keep his eyes unfocused as he slowly opened and closed them.

'Hey, Mika,' called the man. 'Come and look at this one a minute. He looks like our man.'

'Yeah, you're right,' agreed his partner. 'And the fella next to him looks like the other one.'

They both now turned their attention to Dario.

'They look so real, don't they?'

The second man raised his forefinger and moved it towards Dario's forehead. Raffi's muscles tensed. He got ready to run.

'If you touch them, you'll have to pay for them,' came a sharp voice from behind.

The man paused, his fingernail millimetres from Dario's skin.

'Those are metamorphic volumetric displays. They change shape when any physical pressure is applied. Your finger will distort the voxels. Please don't touch!'

Quick footsteps approached. Raffi risked a glance upwards as both men rose to their feet and turned to face an angry-looking Parsim Pennyminder. 'Now would you mind telling me exactly what you want? As you can see, I'm very busy.' He gestured at the customer he had left waiting.

'Two of those things look like the fugitives we're after,' said one of the men.

'Of course they do!' scowled Parsim. 'I mocked them up this morning as a publicity stunt. I was just about to put them in the store window when the customer came in. Now if there's nothing else, I'd really like to get back to her.'

One of the chrono-sans frowned. He glanced back at Dario and Raffi in time to see Dario turning his head and winking at Raffi. Dario froze in that position, then slowly rotated his head back to face front.

'Hold on a minute…' The man looked suspicious.

'Yes, they can move as well,' said Parsim, as if explaining something to a child. He looked sharply at Dario.

'Very clever,' said the other chrono-san. 'But we can't allow it. This is not a game, mister. These young men are dangerous renegades, and we don't want the likes of you giving them cult status. I order you to melt down those heads, or whatever you do with them, immediately. If I come back in here tomorrow and they're still here, we'll close down your store and put you in for six months of Re-Ed.'

The chrono-sans left soon after that, followed immediately by the customer. She had listened in to the end of the conversation and had decided she wanted nothing more to do with a store that mocked up heads of dangerous criminals for publicity. When they were alone, Parsim beckoned to the lads to follow him into his back office. The room, in contrast to the clean, white, minimalist look of the store, was cluttered and untidy in a homely sort of way. The remains of a breakfast competed for desk space with a lapcom keyboard and various bottles and jars.

'So, boys, what took you?' he said to them, closing the door. 'I've been expecting you all morning – ever since they put your faces up all over the Sphere.'

Raffi took one look at the man's crafty grin and twinkling eyes beneath the large dome of his balding head, and he knew they'd come to the right place.

'We're sorry for getting you into trouble, Mr Pennyminder,' said Dario.

'And for losing you a customer,' added Raffi.

Parsim waved their apologies away. 'Don't worry. Those chrono-sans are just bullies. As for the customer, she wasn't going to buy anyway.'

He invited them to sit on a large, well-worn sofa, while he faced them, half seated on the one empty corner of his desk. 'We haven't got much time, boys,' he said to them. 'Those two in here just now were just the start of it. There'll be chrono-sans and police droids all over the Sphere looking for you right now. You have no choice but to change your appearance, and you've come to the right place for that!'

Dario was fiddling with a control panel he'd found on the sofa. He was moving the dial one way and the other, causing the features of a nearby holo-head to change in dramatic ways. He enlarged the nose, mouth and ears to grotesque proportions, then shrank them down so the face became almost nothing but cheeks, chin and forehead.

'As I see it,' continued Parsim, 'you have three options. The first, and most radical, would be surgery: actually changing the bone and tissue of your faces to make you look like the boys whose biometrics you already possess. That would be effective, but may be problematic if you ever leave the Sphere. You would need to find a surgeon out there who could reverse the procedure, or else your mothers would never recognise you. Pay attention, Christo!'

Dario put down the control panel and grinned apologetically.

Satisfied, Parsim continued: 'I would supply you with high-resolution holoscan files that you could present to the surgeon. This would provide all the specifications they require to do the job, but there is always the risk that they may not be able to restore you to exactly the way you are now.'

Parsim had the slow, emphatic speaking style of an experienced commercial medic, looking them both in the eye as he explained things to them. 'Psychologically there are also risks,' he went on. 'You may begin to lose your own sense of identity as the new face becomes familiar to you. You may even find yourselves turning into the people you are impersonating, which could prove problematic if you ever run into your originals. For these reasons, and also the cost, which is considerable, I would steer you away from the surgery option.'

Raffi breathed a sigh of relief. After his experience with Septimus, he'd had quite enough of surgery.

'A second, slightly cheaper option,' said Parsim, 'would be for me to construct each of you a mask.' He pressed a button on his lapcom keyboard and a disembodied hologrammatic face began circulating in the air before them. 'These days, masks are very real-looking: we use lab-grown invitrotissue that looks and feels like the real thing. They are comfortable to wear and adhere well to your face, so there's little chance of them becoming dislodged. You will, however, need to remove them at night to give your facial skin some relief, and I'm not sure how you'd explain that one to your MAIDs.'

Raffi was reminded of Brigitte. He wondered what battles must currently be raging inside her artificial brain. Now that he'd officially become a wanted man, surely she could no longer evade her responsibility to report her suspicions. And yet she was already compromised – they would wonder why she hadn't reported him before. And was her romantic infatuation with him enough to dissuade her from doing her duty to the corporation? Could he risk going back to his dom? It would be a greater risk not to, he decided. If he failed to reappear, Brigitte would have nothing to lose and would almost certainly report him – in which case, a Michael Storm mask would do him no good at all, as it would be Michael Storm they'd be looking for.

'This brings me,' continued Parsim, 'to the third and, to my mind, the most appropriate option for your needs. It's a fairly new process known as Cognitive Inference Deception, or CID. It exploits the fact that our sense of vision arises not from the information coming through our eyes but on the interpretation of this information by the brain. As the information coming through our eyes is actually fairly poor, the brain must often make assumptions about what we're looking at, based on expectation or previous experience. But the brain can sometimes be fooled into thinking it's seeing something it isn't. This is the case with optical illusions such as the never-ending staircase or the many tricks that make lines appear to bend or circles seem bigger or smaller than they are. Now, thanks to CID, we can also fool the eye and brain with faces.'

He looked at them both with calm, almost hypnotic authority. 'So how does it work?' he asked them rhetorically. 'Put simply, CID is a mask made of light pixels. The pixels are so arranged that, when perceived by an observer, they collectively form an unresolved picture of a face that must then be interpreted by the brain according to its particular expectations. Effectively this means that when people look at you, they see what they expect to see. Strangers will see a normal, anonymous human face – two eyes, a nose and a mouth – and each of them will construct that face differently. It's the most perfect means yet devised for 'blending in', as no two witnesses will ever describe you in the same way. Only your friends will be able to see you as you really look.'

Raffi and Dario stared at each other.

'This could do the trick,' said Dario after a moment's pause.

'What about androids?' asked Raffi.

'Most androids have pretty basic machine vision. They have sufficient light, depth and motion perception to allow themselves to move around without bumping into things, but nothing more sophisticated than that. Of more concern are the hovercams you sometimes see flying around the place. CID can fool most of these because, like the human eye, their vision is based on interpretation of the limited information coming through their lenses. But there are more sophisticated ones around now that can override CID. These are already in use at the Sphere's exit points.'

'You're saying we can't escape the Sphere, even using CID?'

Parsim shook his head 'You couldn't leave the Sphere with a traditional mask on either. The infrared imaging scanners would spot it immediately. If you're really set on leaving, your only hope is surgery.'

Raffi gulped. 'I couldn't face that!'

'Accept it, mate,' said Dario. 'We're not leaving – at least not yet.' He turned to Parsim. 'How much would the CID treatment cost, Mr Pennyminder?'

'Five thousand u-dolls per mask.'

'Jeebus!' Dario frowned. 'I don't think Christo's got that sort of money. Can I pay in installments?'

'Wait,' said Raffi, hurriedly trying to reassess their situation. 'What about people we know but can't trust, like Red? He'll see through the CID, won't he?'

'There you go again, mate! Red's cool, I keep telling you.'

Raffi turned on Dario. 'He's not cool, Christo, believe me! He's hated me ever since I beat him in that race. He's praying for a chance to destroy me. And if Lastara is now his girlfriend, we can't trust her any more either–'

'It's not a problem, my boy,' interrupted Parsim. 'It works on expectations, remember? If – before this Red fellow catches sight of you – one of your trusted friends introduces you as Michael Storm, Red will see you as Michael Storm. Or – if he doesn't already know Michael Storm – his brain will construct a face that, from then on, will be Michael Storm for him.'

Dario smiled. For him the decision was made. Even Raffi had to accept that CID was their best hope. Pennyminder wouldn't offer Dario credit. 'Forgive me,' he explained to Dario, 'but in your precarious circumstances, I can't be sure if you would ever be able to complete the payments.'

Luckily Michael Storm had quite deep pockets, and Raffi was able to pay for both CID masks.

The CID masks, being generic, were quick to create and install.

'I can't feel a thing,' said Dario when the process was complete. Raffi, examining himself in the mirror, couldn't believe he was even wearing it. He looked exactly the same as before.

'You expect to see your own face in there, so that's what you see,' explained Parsim. 'A stranger looking at you now would see a quite different face.'

Raffi touched his face and felt only his bare skin. 'Where's the mask? Why can't I feel it?'

'The technical term for it,' said Parsim, 'is an autostereoscopic spatially multiplexed parallax display. It exists as a light field that's shaped to fit the contours of your face. You can't feel it any more than you can feel a ray of moonlight, but it's there, I assure you.'

CHAPTER TWENTY-THREE

⏳

CALENDAR SQUARE

O n leaving Parsim's store, Raffi and Dario headed off for a game of air-tennis. Their faces stared down at them from hover-hoardings above every street, yet they didn't attract attention from anyone, including the gyndroid at the tenniplex reception desk. Buoyed by their ionic propulsor hover-heels, the boys flew around the court for an energetic hour, serving, returning, lobbing and smashing the ball over the six-metre-high net. Dario beat Raffi by more than the usual margin. Raffi found he was constantly over-hitting – nerves, probably. Dario seemed calmer, better able to deal with their new circumstances. 'We have to act normally,' he advised Raffi before the game. 'Our masks will help, but we can't afford to call attention to ourselves in any way at all.' After they'd showered and changed, Dario called Jonah and asked him to meet them on nearby Interim Arcade.

'Are you sure?' queried Jonah. He must have seen the 'wanted' signs everywhere.

'Trust us!' said Dario.

'I'm due to meet Lastara on Calendar Square in half an hour. Can we meet there instead?'

They agreed to meet Jonah at the central fountain on Calendar Square. He arrived there ten minutes after they did, sending a small group of pigeons scattering as he landed. He looked up at them in alarm as he removed his helmet. 'Hey, shouldn't you two be wearing a disguise?'

'Relax,' beamed Dario. 'No one's going to recognise us.' Jonah shook his head in wonder as the mysteries of the CID masks were revealed to him. 'You're going to have to introduce us as Michael Storm and Christo Ellis,' Dario added. 'Michael's worried about Lastara and Red, for some reason.'

'I don't trust him – or her now,' said Raffi. 'I think they might just blab to Secrocon when they see us. But if you can introduce us as Michael Storm and Christo Ellis when you see Lastara, her brain'll construct a different set of faces for us.'

'You're wrong about her, Mike,' said Jonah. 'Lastara's totally trustworthy. She won't blab to anyone. She's part of the gang, isn't she? You wait and see. It'll be fine.'

'That's what I keep telling him,' said Dario.

Raffi was about to respond, but was interrupted by the barking of a dog somewhere close by, followed by a loud clatter of wings as a flock of birds exploded out of a tree. Then his eye was caught by something across the square, out of Dario and Jonah's field of vision. He saw a lingerie store called Satin Secrets. The people inside it were motionless like store mannequins, imprisoned in their own particular present as the world moved on around them. All except for one. She was tall, radiant, blonde, and instantly familiar. Lastara was standing near the store entrance, cradling a dilator in her left hand. With her right she pressed something on her pale metallic blue belt and a hole appeared in the floor beneath a young female store assistant. The frozen girl fell through it and the floor reappeared above her. Lastara made a quick visual check of the scene outside the store. No one was looking her way – no one except Raffi, and he was below her eye level and partly obscured by the fountain. Her eyes were hooded and her cherubic lips were smiling, as if she was welcoming the first ecstatic wave of a new paradisiac into her system. In one smooth movement she shut down the dilator and pushed it into her bag before heading off into the crowds. As people in the store began moving again, and puzzling over the sudden disappearance of the store girl, Lastara sailed gracefully away from the scene, half a head taller than most, conspicuously beautiful, and for that reason the last person anyone would suspect of the crime.

'You okay, Mike?' asked Jonah. His voice seemed to arrive from another dimension.

Raffi shook his head and shut his gaping mouth. 'You won't believe what I just saw,' he said. 'Lastara was in that store just over there.' They both turned to see where he was pointing. 'She used a dilator to freeze everyone, then she pressed this button on her belt and a hole opened up in the floor and a young store girl disappeared through it. Then Lastara just left. I lost her in the crowd somewhere over there.'

'Mate, is the heat getting to you or something?' scoffed Dario. 'That's the looniest thing I ever heard.'

Jonah looked furious. 'I expected better of you, Mike. I know you don't like Lastara, but I didn't think you'd be prepared to make up stories about her.'

'I'd be the first to admit Lastara can be a pain,' put in Dario. 'She's a vain, selfish, narcissistic, head-in-the-sand junkie of the first order. But no way in hooly is she the kidnapper. You're off beam again, mate.'

'First he was accusing you, Dario. Now he's trying to pin it on Lastara. Who's next in our gang, Mike? Is Sal going to be the kidnapper? Or me?' Jonah looked about ready to explode with anger. Raffi was too shocked and upset to say anything.

'Is that the store girl you mean?' asked Dario, pointing. Raffi looked back towards the store. The girl he'd seen not two minutes earlier falling through the hole in the floor was now back behind her counter, serving customers. Everything looked perfectly normal. The girl and the customers she was serving didn't look the least bit puzzled or upset by what he'd seen just happen.

'That's her,' Raffi breathed. 'I can't understand it.' For a moment, he wondered if he was going mad. Then he caught sight of a flash of blond hair moving through the crowds from the right. He grabbed Dario's arm. 'I think it must have been a Rezzy Flash,' he said. 'Now watch! Both of you!'

They turned once more to look as Lastara entered Satin Secrets, removed the dilator from her bag and fired a wide-beam cone of light at the store interior. The customers and store girl stopped in mid-action as the beam struck. In a different part of the square, a dog barked and a flock of birds exploded out of a tree. Raffi observed Jonah and Dario – especially Jonah – as they watched the events unfold in the store. In less than twenty seconds, the show was over, and Lastara moved gracefully off stage.

Neither Jonah nor Dario spoke as they watched her leave and the bewildered expression form on the face of the female customer as the store girl who had just been serving her disappeared before her eyes. She and the other customers looked confused, then anxious and fearful. They had all heard tales of young people disappearing, but had perhaps never fully believed them – certainly never expected to witness a disappearance.

Without saying a word to Raffi or Dario, Jonah ran through the crowds to the store. He talked to the customer who had last seen the girl, then spoke into his wearable. Within less than a minute – almost as if it had been waiting for the call – a blue-flashing airsearcher descended into the square outside Satin Secrets. A small crowd gathered outside the store entrance. Raffi heard no anger and little surprise in the voices around him, just a thrum of low, urgent mutterings: Poor girl! What a terrible thing! Must tell so-and-so. People here, he decided, liked to read their copies of Tower Times and go on believing that everything was fine. These disappearances were of brief, anecdotal interest, but very quickly forgotten – always young people, please note, and always young people unaccompanied by parents or guardians. The witness gave her description, and the airsearcher took off again. Raffi suspected that it simply headed back to wherever it came from.

'I'm sorry, mate,' said Dario quietly as they watched all this. 'You were right this time.'

'I take no pleasure in it,' murmured Raffi. 'I just hope Jonah's okay.'

They watched as their friend slowly returned. 'How did you know she was going to do that?' Jonah asked.

'Botched resynchronisation,' explained Raffi. 'I sometimes get short flashes of the future.'

'Well, then I'm sorry. I shouldn't have said those things to you.'

'No worries, Jonah. You okay?'

He looked nervous. 'You won't let on that you saw this, will you?'

'You mean to Sal?'

'I mean to Lastara.'

'No,' said Raffi. 'For the simple reason that I never want to see her again. I think you should wash your hands of her, too, Jonah. You have to wonder how many of the other kidnappings were done by her. The one on Tomorrow and Third – I thought it had to be Dario. And then when I realised I was wrong about that, I thought it must have been Red. But none of us thought about Lastara. She was there in the store all the time. We assumed she was trying on an outfit, but–' He stopped, pulled up sharp by the expression on Jonah's face. 'Don't tell me you still feel the same way about her.'

'Don't hate her,' said Jonah.

Raffi looked at him. 'Well what am I supposed to feel about someone who does what she just did? She must be working for Secrocon, sending these kids to be time-locked and tortured by that maniac Avon Drak. No wonder she's always the first to defend Secrocon whenever we have those conversations. She's the enemy, Jonah. You can't carry on being friends with her and with us. You have to choose.'

'She doesn't like Secrocon any more than you do, Mike.'

'Then why's she doing this?'

'She needs the money.'

Raffi almost laughed. 'You've got to be kidding. She's a top e-mag model about to launch herself in the reality-soaps. How can she be short of money?'

Jonah looked away. 'You don't know the whole story, Mike. You only ever see what's on the surface, and you're always so quick to judge!'

Raffi felt as though he'd been hit in the throat. 'Did you see what I just saw, Jonah? And you're defending her? Back me up, Dario.'

Dario shrugged. 'I have to concur with Michael on this one, Jonah, mate. I know you and Lastara go way back, but you have to see she's gone over to the dark side. There's no other way of explaining what we all just saw.'

'She's in a desperate state,' said Jonah. 'She needs to be

helped, not cast out. Look, I'm going to talk to her. I've tried to before, but–'

'Before? You mean you knew about this?'

Jonah looked terrified. 'No. Well, I suspected. After Tomorrow and Third, I started to think about it and I kind of reached the conclusion you just came to. She was always there or thereabouts when these things happened. Look, she's short of money. She swore me to secrecy on this, but I suppose I'll have to tell you. The modelling work has dried up. These days, fashion houses tend to use gyndroids – they're cheaper and, okay, Lastara can be a bit fussy about working conditions at times, whereas gyndroids never complain. As for her reality-soap ambitions, well take it from me, it's never going to happen. Even I can see that Lastara can't act. But she's got expensive needs. She likes her pills, you know. I try to help her with money when I can, but the funds are running low.'

'Well why doesn't she get a job then?' Raffi demanded. 'You know, a normal kind of job. She could work in one of these stores instead of kidnapping their staff.'

Dario laughed. 'Lastara? Work in a store? You've got to be kidding, mate.'

Raffi couldn't bring himself to share Dario's amusement.

'She's been in here a long time, that's all I'll say,' said Jonah. 'This place, the Chronosphere, it's alright for a while, but if you stay here too long... It made me sick in the body. I think it's made Lastara a bit sick in the mind.'

'The Moon Effect, you mean?'

'Maybe. I don't know. I don't think anyone knows. But we're living life at an unnatural speed. Perhaps our bodies and minds just aren't built for it. Maybe in the future, as generations of new kids grow up in this world, humans will evolve to thrive in these conditions. But for us pioneers there are always going to be problems. Just don't judge us too harshly. Even the machines are struggling. I've heard rumours that some of the domicile MAIDs are developing personality disorders. The trouble is, this is all so new, even for the scientists. They had no way of measuring the long-term effects. We're all basically rats in one big lab experiment.'

CHAPTER TWENTY-FOUR

⧗

A WORLD OF TROUBLE

'Raphael Delgado! Dario Brice! What do you know?' Red's unmistakably refined tones echoed around the square.

Raffi wanted to run and hide, but there was nowhere to go. The squat cyborg had landed in the square no more than five metres from them, legs astride his hoverbike, and staring right at them.

Jonah tried to intervene. 'Red!' he cried in a panicked welcome. 'Have you met Michael Storm and Christo Ellis? They're old friends of mine.'

Red blinked and rubbed his telescopically enhanced eyes, but Raffi could see he wasn't going to be fooled. Having recognised them first time round, the CID masks could do nothing more than confirm him in his identification. 'So that's what you're calling yourselves these days? I don't know how you chaps expect to get away with this. Your faces are all over the Sphere. You're going to get spotted any minute now and sent back where you belong.'

Raffi saw the frown of disappointment in Dario's face – he hadn't expected this from someone he'd thought of as a mate.

Red was talking too loudly. Soon he would start attracting unwelcome attention.

'You must be Red Oakes,' said Raffi quickly. 'Jonah's told us about you. Listen, we were just about to have a picnic lunch in Tomorrow Fields. Would you like to join us?'

Red ignored him and spoke to Dario. 'I expected more intelligence from you, old chap. But then again, choosing morons like Delgado for company, perhaps you're not as bright as I gave you credit for.' Then he turned to Raffi. 'To answer your question, moron: the answer's no, I shall not be joining you for lunch. I don't make a habit of fraternising with escaped convicts.' He began opening his throttle in preparation for flight when he was checked by a shout.

'Red! Oh, there you are sweetheart.' Lastara came charging through the lunchtime crowds. She lifted Red's visor and leaned down to plant a kiss on his craggy cheek.

Raffi glared meaningfully at Jonah, who then sprang forward. 'Lastara. Hi there!'

'Oh, hello dearie. I didn't expect to see you just yet.'

'Meet my friends Michael Storm and Christo Ellis.'

She looked up. A moment of uncertainty clouded the exotic topaz of her eyes. 'You look familiar,' she murmured to Dario. 'Have we...'

'Of course he looks familiar,' roared Red. 'That's your ex you're looking at, Dario Brice. And that one's Raffi Delgado. For Bo-sakes, can't you recognise them?'

'But...' Lastara looked confused. With her mind struggling to resolve competing expectations of what she was seeing, Raffi wondered exactly what the CID masks were currently showing her.

'Red's wrong,' said Jonah. 'He must be confused.'

Raffi looked at Dario quizzically. 'Do you know what he's going on about? Who are these people, Darius Brice and Raffa Delgado?'

'Search me,' mugged Dario, hamming it up perhaps a little too much.

Their three-pronged effort was enough to win the day against Red. Lastara held her hand out for Dario and then Raffi to shake. Raffi couldn't fail to notice how she made eyes at Dario, as she tended to do at all good-looking strangers. She must have constructed his face in a very eye-pleasing way.

Seeing this, Red's face contorted into an ugly fusion of outrage, bewilderment and jealousy. Uttering a cry of exasperation, he opened up his throttle, took his foot off the air brake and soared rapidly skywards.

Lastara turned. 'Now where's he got to? We were supposed to be having lunch.' Shrugging, she looked back at Dario and smiled coquettishly. 'Oh well, in that case, I shall just have to make do with you boys.'

⧖

They dined at Pierre Chang's, a Sino-French eathouse on Season and Sixth, taking an indoor table to get out of the heat. It was an awkward affair – at least for Raffi, who couldn't look at or listen to Lastara without recalling what he'd seen her do earlier in Satin Secrets. It was difficult to ignore her, however, as she regaled them with an account of her fashion shoot that morning and how the art director spent the whole time flirting with her. Raffi toyed distractedly with his peking duck pancake wrap. It came with a small syringe of thermomixed hoisin sauce, which he felt at times like squirting in her face while declaring her a liar. Meanwhile Jonah smiled and laughed, and Raffi wondered how he could listen to such garbage knowing it was all just an insane girl's fantasies. You weren't at a fashion shoot, he wanted to scream at her. You were kidnapping a store girl for Secrocon. But he bit his tongue for Jonah's sake.

Then, over dessert (tarte tatin with foam of custard), something snapped in him. Lastara was talking about an acting job she was due to audition for in which she would have to appear in some sexy underwear. She told them she'd gone to her favourite lingerie store in Calendar Square to check out what they had.

'Oh yes, we saw you in there earlier,' interrupted Raffi. 'Satin Secrets, wasn't it?' He felt Jonah tense up beside him. Dario, seated opposite, flashed his eyes at him in warning, but Raffi couldn't help himself. 'You dilated the whole place, then sent the store assistant dropping through a hole in the floor, didn't you?'

Lastara looked at him, her golden skin turning pale before his eyes while her lips moved soundlessly.

'That must have been someone else, mate!' chuckled Dario nervously.

'Yeah, that couldn't have been Lastara,' murmured Jonah, the edges of his nostrils white with rage and tension.

What a spell she weaves over her men, thought Raffi despairingly.

'I don't know what sort of person would do such a thing,' said Lastara at last. She was smiling, but not with her usual self-confidence. Raffi was pleased to have pierced, even briefly, that cocoon of fantasy she had carefully constructed around herself.

Back at his domicile, Raffi nervously pressed his index finger to the scanpad and waited for the door to click open. He couldn't predict what Brigitte's attitude might be. She may have already notified Secrocon, in which case...

Standing in the small entrance corridor – almost filling it up with his bulky frame – was Chrono-San Shep Tallis.

Raffi's immediate instinct was to make a run for it. But that, the more intelligent part of him quickly pointed out, would be worse than futile: it would actually invite suspicion. Instead he returned the smile as best he could. 'Hello, officer.'

'Good afternoon, young man. How are you today?'

'Very well, thanks. How can I help you?'

'Been out enjoying the fine weather, have we?'

This, in a place of perpetual summer, was obviously meant as a joke, either to put him at ease or – more likely – to do the opposite.

Raffi simply nodded. Tallis was acting like he knew something – like he knew everything. Did he even know about the CID mask? Was he just playing him along like a fat, lazy cat toying with a rodent?

'Come in, come in,' smiled Tallis. 'Don't let me keep you trapped in your own hallway. Raffi followed the chrono-san into his tiny living room. The big man gestured for Raffi to take a chair, while he reclined on the more comfortable sofa, running a hand over his cropped grey hair. 'Brigitte,' he called, 'be a honey and make us both a cup of tea. Hot and white.'

'Certainly, chrono-san,' said Brigitte with just a hint of warm flirtatiousness in her vocal timbre. Their evident chumminess caused Raffi to ponder how long Tallis had already been here and how much she'd said to him.

Two wheeled menials, each supporting a mug of steaming tea, glided out of the kitchen and came to rest next to Raffi and Tallis. Narrow legs telescoped downwards from beneath flat upper surfaces, turning them into occasional tables with height set for easy reachability.

Tallis examined Raffi carefully as he sipped his tea. 'What d'you know about a Mr Rupert Oakes?' he asked finally.

Raffi had never heard Red's given name before, but knew Tallis could mean no other. The rat must have called the

Police Centre as soon as he'd left them. Be careful now, he told himself: cameras may well have recorded images of him and Red in Calendar Square, so it wouldn't do to deny it: 'I met someone called Red Oakes earlier today. Is that who you mean?'

'That's the one.'

'What about him?'

'He claims he met the dangerous kidnapper Raphael Delgado in Calendar Square this afternoon.'

'Yes, I remember! He thought I was Delgado!'

Tallis frowned. 'And why do you suppose he thought that?'

'I've no idea.'

'Is it possible that when Mr Oakes first met the kidnapper, he was posing as you? Could that be why he's mixing the two of you up?'

'Maybe. I just don't know.'

'Do you know Delgado?'

'No.' As Raffi said this, he remembered having told Brigitte that Raffi was a friend. She must know now that he was lying to the chrono-san, and yet she said nothing. Scared, maybe, of implicating herself.

'I should remind you, Mr Storm, that aiding and abetting a fugitive is a punishable offence. The Chronosphere is a wonderful holiday resort, but it's also a self-contained society with is own laws and regulations. That's an inevitable consequence of our time-isolated existence. We have to get tough with the lawbreakers in order to allow good chrononauts to enjoy a safe and secure voyage. That's the job of chrono-sans like myself. If you behave well, you shouldn't ever need to see or hear from us. But if you don't, believe me, we can make a world of trouble for you… Now I'll ask you again: do you know, or have you ever known, Raphael Delgado?'

'No.'

Tallis put down his mug and stood up. 'Well, thank you for your time, Mr Storm... Don't get up. I can see myself out.' He looked back from the hallway. 'Do remember to give me a call if you remember anything about Delgado or Brice. And thank you Brigitte,' he called out as he left. 'You make a helluva nice cup of tea!'

'I've missed you, Michael,' said Brigitte, when they were alone. Raffi didn't need to check her personality settings to know they were back at their extreme positions. Through the doorway of his bedroom he could see the familiar black sphere squatting in its usual corner. 'Do you want to spend a little quality time with me?' This was payback, he realised: she had lied for him – lied by omission, anyway. And she was probably scared – or the machine equivalent – knowing she was now as implicated in this whole thing as he was. Without a word, he walked into the bedroom, stepped through the little hatchway and slid into the cosy darkness of the virtuarium.

The following morning, Brigitte was her usual friendly and efficient self. There was no mention of anything that had occurred the day before. Later, Raffi rode waves on Lake Perpetuity, had lunch with Dario at Atomic Sands, hung out at the virtu-real games arcade on Tomorrow and Third, then met up with Sal for an evening at the holoplex on Season Square – in short, it was a perfectly normal Chronospheric day. The only place he didn't dare go was the Hover Track Arena on Solstice and Fourth, not wanting to risk running into Red again. There were no further visits from the police that day or the next, and as time began to slip uneventfully by, Raffi gradually relaxed. Against all the odds, his new life as Michael Storm seemed to be working out.

A pattern emerged in his relationship with Brigitte. Every day at sundown, her personality would shift to its most extreme settings, and she would evolve into a sentimental, lovelorn and romantically demanding version of her normal self. Each evening, no matter what time Raffi returned home, she would invite him to join her in the virtuarium. Once he was installed in its harness, she would appear to him as a lookalike of Anna Morrow through whose beautifully constructed lips she would bombard him with long, cod-poetic expressions of adoration. These performances would take place against a succession of evocative backdrops – a moon-washed beach; a twilit desert encampment; or the chilly parapet of a castle ruin at dawn. Then, at some point, they would start to kiss, and the smell and touch and taste of these kisses, and the feel of her body beneath his caresses, felt remarkably real – so much so that Raffi almost began to look forward to these moments. When they had finished making love, Brigitte would subside into a deep and fulfilled standby, and Raffi would himself start to nod off, often spending the whole night asleep in the virtuarium. Brigitte would wake him with breakfast and the courteous tone of any healthy domicile MAID, as if the night before, and all the previous nights before, had never happened.

It was okay, wasn't it? He could live like this without too much trouble? Well, almost. At the back of Raffi's mind as he climbed through the virtuarium hatchway each evening, and then again much stronger when he awoke each morning, there was the guilt – guilt that he was prepared to pollute the sacred memory of that sad and lonely girl for his own sordid pleasure. Sometimes he toyed with the idea of replacing her with someone else – swapping those treasured features with those of someone who could be trusted to provoke mere sensual pleasure – but when it came down to it, he could never bring himself to ask Brigitte to tweak a single pixel of Miss Morrow's lovingly reconstructed form.

Days turned into weeks. The weather remained warm – just less than uncomfortably so. Raffi continued to spend time with Dario and Sal, although he saw much less of Jonah. The incident on Calendar Square had exposed a major faultline in their friendship – a faultline bearing the unmistakable shape of Lastara Blue: Jonah couldn't let go of her, while Raffi hoped never to set eyes on her again. Worse, Jonah's willingness to overlook her flaws – and even the fact that she was working for Secrocon – struck Raffi as a major character flaw. While he'd once marvelled at the lad's devotion, now he just saw it as willful blindness, and pitied him for it. Another reason for Raffi steering clear of Lastara, apart from her being hateful to his sight, was her continuing relationship with Red Oakes, which Raffi heard about through Sal. Red never admitted to reporting them to Secrocon, but he hadn't changed his mind about what he'd seen either, resulting in an uneasy stalemate: as Raffi understood it from Sal, so long as he and Dario kept out of Red's sight, Red would stay quiet about them. So the gang was beginning to disintegrate, with Raffi and Dario going one way, Jonah and Lastara going the other, and Sal of all people acting as the only bridge between them.

CHAPTER TWENTY-FIVE

Logic Dictates...

One morning, in the seventh month of Raffi's chronospheric year, a stranger entered his domicile. Raffi was in the kitchen at the time. He'd just finished a late breakfast and was idly flicking through the sensovision channels, wondering what he was going to do with himself. With fewer friends and the loss of hoverbike racing as a leisure activity, he was finding his days getting somewhat harder to fill.

The sound of a footstep in the entrance hall made him look up. Through the doorway he saw a young man staring at him. He was about 18, tall and slim with dark hair – much like Raffi in almost every way, even down to the shocked look on his face.

'Who are you?' the young man demanded. 'What are you doing in my dom?'

In a flash of understanding, Raffi knew what was going on. Stay calm, he urged himself, fighting back the growing sense of panic. The important thing was to get out before

Brigitte woke up to the situation and called the authorities. He darted out of the kitchen, brushing past the boy, and walked to the door. The handle wouldn't move. Damn!

'B?' he said urgently. 'Can you open the door.'

'I cannot, Michael,' she answered. 'You see, I am confused.'

Raffi closed his eyes, leaning his forehead against the door. The game was well and truly up.

'That makes two of us,' he heard the boy say angrily. 'B, why in hooly are you suddenly calling this guy Michael? What's going on around here, B?'

There was a faint crackle and hiss behind her next words, which she seemed to have some trouble expressing. 'Michael, my sensors suggest that there are now two of you. Logic dictates that cannot be so. Therefore one of you must be... an imposter.'

'Yeah, him!' said the boy. 'Look at him, B. He doesn't look a thing like me.'

'My visual sensors are poor,' B confessed. 'Outward appearance, anyway, is a poor gauge of identity. Humans often change in appearance. We are programmed to identify customers by their biometric data. You both have identical biometric data.'

Raffi blinked, and turned to face the boy. Maybe he still had half a chance of surviving this. He'd assumed that the return of the genuine Michael Storm would have sent Brigitte's joy receptors into overdrive. She had never fully accepted or trusted Raffi's impersonation of him, and her suspicions were now surely vindicated. So why was she hesitating? Could it be that she was scared of Raffi – of what he might reveal about her? And could that fear be enough to outweigh her desire to embrace her long-lost lover?

The boy was glaring at him. 'You little creep! I step outside for half a minute to top up my account and you come along and steal my identity. You'll never get away with this, you bastard. I'll tell Secrocon.'

Moving more purposefully now, Raffi approached the boy and looked at him appraisingly, in the way he remembered Shep Tallis had studied him earlier. 'How did you expect to pull this one off, friend?' he asked quietly. 'If you want to pretend to be someone else, it's not enough just to get some surgery done on your eyes and fingers. You've got to get rid of the guy, too.' Raffi looked up, as he often did, quite needlessly, when addressing Brigitte. 'What shall we do with him, B? Shall we call Secrocon? Or shall we give him one hour to get the hell out of the Sphere?'

He could see he'd made Michael nervous. His bravado looked forced. 'Yeah!' the young man challenged. 'Go on then. Call Secrocon. I'll prove to them in two minutes that I'm me. There's plenty they know about me that you don't. Come to that, there's plenty B knows about me that you don't – like what part of Londaris I come from. I've talked about it with you loads, haven't I, B? Go on then, mister. Say it. Where do I come from?'

It was Raffi's turn to feel pushed onto the back foot. He had to come up with something, and fast, to avoid sounding like the faker. Random place names flashed into his head: Sky City, Temside, Old London, New Canterbury. 'Foxton,' he hazarded, guessing there was something of the seaside in the lad's rough and ruddy complexion.

The young man chortled triumphantly. 'Wrong! So completely, hilariously wrong.' He turned his face upwards, as Raffi had done earlier. 'Tell him, B. Tell him where I come from, and then we can call in the chrono-sans and get rid of this lying idiot.'

'From Foxton,' said Brigitte simply. 'Michael comes from Foxton.'

Raffi began breathing again. She was scared. In fact, she

was terrified. She'd worked out that if she exposed Raffi, he would have nothing to lose and would tell the authorities everything. The return of Michael Storm was as bad for her as it was for him.

The boy looked like he'd just been slapped. 'What's got into you, B?' he whined. 'I come from Mandelsea. You know that!' He scratched his head a little desperately. 'Okay. Okay then. What's my favourite band? Come on! They played Periodic Park the first week I was here.' He tilted his head towards the ceiling. 'You keep quiet now, B. No helping him, yeah?'

'Dark Entropy,' said Raffi.

'Wrong again! See? I hate Dark Entropy, don't I, B? Don't I?' Michael Storm was almost dancing now. 'My favourite band is Firebird, yeah?'

'Your favourite band may well be Firebird,' said Brigitte. 'But Michael Storm's is Dark Entropy. And that was the band he went to see in his first week in the Sphere.'

'Shit! You're talking shit, B. And you know it. What's this guy got on you, huh? What's he done to you that you can deny me, deny everything?' He turned to Raffi. 'You've done something, haven't you? You've fiddled with her. I'm calling the Tech Centre.' He strode towards the bedroom, heading for the bedside handcom. 'I'm going to get to the bottom of th–'

Something happened then, almost too quickly for Raffi to process it. Just as Michael was passing the kitchen doorway and about to enter the bedroom, a projectile – something small and dark – flew out and struck him. And now the boy was crouching down, clutching his head and moaning. The object, a humble teaspoon, lay on the carpet by his feet.

'There is nothing wrong with me,' said Brigitte calmly, with just a hint of hiss and crackle in her voice. 'There is no need to call the Tech Centre.'

Raffi caught Michael's eye. 'Get out!' he whispered through gritted teeth. 'While you still have a chance, get out!' He placed his forefinger to his temple and made circles with it, the age-old gesture for madness, which he hoped hadn't yet entered the MAID's ever-growing vocabulary of signs and symbols.

'I'm not going anywhere,' gasped Michael weakly. Still holding his head, he moved into the bedroom. A menial swiftly entered the room behind him bearing a cup of steaming water. The miniature wheeled robot barged into Michael's calves, upending the cup and splashing the water all over his legs.

He screamed. 'What the–! Aaaagh.' He kicked the menial across the room so that it smashed into the wall. Groaning, he fell on the bed and ripped off his trousers. When his hands were free again he grabbed the handcom and pressed T. 'Tech Centre. Tech Centre. I've got an emergency. My MAID's gone –' He stopped talking then and his eyes bulged as he saw what was coming towards him on board a second menial, which had just emerged from the kitchen. Raffi recognized it as a meat slicer, its long, serrated-edge blade buzzing and moving back and forth in a manic rhythm.

Michael wriggled higher up onto the bed so that his legs were clear of the floor. 'Help,' he cried. 'Oh shit! Mummy! Help!'

Raffi snapped out of his mini trance. 'Stop it, Brigitte,' he yelled. 'I order you to stop this at once.'

The menial with its deadly cargo continued to approach the bed.

'There is nothing wrong with me,' said Brigitte matter-of-factly. 'There is no need to call the Tech Centre.'

In another, much calmer voice he heard her addressing the bewildered voice on the handcom. 'I'm sorry for the disturbance. Michael Storm has just suffered a bout of somniloquy. I believe he is having an unpleasant dream. I will suggest that he reduces his consumption of cheese before bedtime.' CLICK.

The buzz of the slicer increased in volume as the menial began awkwardly climbing the side of the bed, using rotating hook-lined tracks built into its legs to cling to the bedspread.

Raffi picked up a chair and brought it down hard on the menial. It fell with a crash to the floor, tracks impotently turning, upturned slicer still angrily buzzing.

He looked at Michael. 'I'm serious,' he murmured. 'You'd better get out of here.'

Michael nodded palely, drained of all words. He quickly got up from the bed, grabbed his trousers, and scarpered for the front door. It was locked, of course. 'Can you get her to open the door?' he pleaded.

'Open the door, Brigitte. Let the lad go. He promises not to come back, don't you?'

Michael nodded.

'And you're not going to call the Tech Centre, are you?'

He shook his head.

'Open the door, B,' Raffi repeated.

'Logic dictates there cannot be two Michaels,' said Brigitte placidly. 'It is… confusion. It is… wrong. Questions will be asked. What happened, B, they will ask me. How did you allow this situation to arise? Is there something wrong, B? No. There is nothing wrong with me. There is no need to call the Tech Centre.'

The boys looked at each other helplessly. More cutlery came flying out of the kitchen, heading straight for Michael. He ducked, but some of it struck him. A fork stuck itself into his side, making him cry out again. Then larger utensils began flying, including a chopping knife that embedded itself into the wall just centimetres from his ear.

Michael began sobbing with fear.

The entrance hall was completely exposed to the artillery fire from the kitchen, so he darted into the bathroom. Bad idea, thought Raffi. Michael soon came screaming out of there, dripping from head to toe in scalding water. Then he began hopping and jumping madly from foot to foot, emitting little cries of pain. Blue sparks were leaping out of the carpet wherever he put his feet.

She's going to kill him, thought Raffi. She seriously means to kill him. He watched dazedly as the poor, bedraggled young man charged into the bedroom and leapt back onto the bed, the only refuge from the merciless electric shocks. He lay curled up and shaking as, with machine-like relentlessness, the slicer-bearing menial righted itself and recommenced its climb up the bed. Raffi bashed it down once more with the chair, but he wondered how long it would be before Brigitte turned on him. Not long, was the answer. A bright zinger pierced his heel, blasting its way through his central nervous system before embedding itself like a quivering spear in his skull. He leapt half a metre, then clambered onto the bed.

'I'm sorry, Michael. But there is nothing wrong with me. There is no need to call the Tech Centre.'

Raffi's head lolled and his eyes closed dopily. He was vaguely aware of Michael crying. 'She's going to kill us,' the young man wept. 'Oh god, she's going to kill us both. See what you did, you idiot. See what you did by pretending to be me. You've made her mad.'

More menials were now trundling into the bedroom, each of them armed with an array of sharp and threatening food-processing equipment: blenders, juicers, mincers, skewers, scrapers, squeezers, graters, grinders – things Raffi barely recognised, things he could hardly believe had a home in a kitchen – flayers, mashers, extruders, extractors, wedgers, cleavers, peelers, crackers.

Sleepily, Raffi eyed the chair. But he didn't fancy another

brain-frying blue spark through the soles of his feet trying to retrieve it. Three of the menials were already climbing up the bed. He tried kicking one off, but the little hooks in its tracks clung on and it soon continued its ascent. The first one to reach the bed's surface bore a propellor-like blender, which suddenly whirred into roaring life and made a bee-line for Michael. The lad pushed at the thing with a pillow, but within seconds it was no more than a cloud of feathers that filled the room like snowflakes. Michael screamed and backed away towards the top of the bed sucking his bleeding knuckle. Raffi cast despairingly around for something he could use for attack or defence. The menials were all queued up like tin soldiers, awaiting their turn to mount the bed. Beyond them was the fallen chair and the table, and to the left of that was the glass sliding door that led to the balcony, the Upper Atrium and freedom.

It was almost impossible to think with the ear-splitting roar of the demon blender, now just centimetres from Michael's splayed toes. Raffi climbed unsteadily to his feet. The bed felt like a big jelly beneath him and his head still throbbed from the electro-shock treatment from the floor. The line of menials before him bristled with sharpened steel.

He stood at the edge of the bed, playing out in his mind exactly where he would have to place his feet. There were perches here and there on the tops of those menials – small and precarious maybe, but they might just support him for the half-second he needed before launching himself towards the next one.

Behind him, Michael was screaming again. That thing was probably eating into his feet by now. Raffi didn't dare look back. Instead he took a deep breath and leapt into space.

CHAPTER TWENTY-SIX

⌛

TROUBLE AT CASTAMORE'S

e landed awkwardly, grazing his ankle skin on a grater and nearly tumbling sideways, but he had just enough momentum for a further bound forwards, this time arriving on a tiny perch at the front of the next menial, where a skewer embedded itself in the toecap of his shoe. This wasn't too bad except that his weight then unbalanced the menial, pitching it forwards. Somehow, he avoided falling with it and kept going, though he no longer had any idea where his feet would end up. An upturned fruit-core extractor nearly penetrated the sole of his shoe on the next landing, and a blow torch burst into blue life on the following one, scorching his shin. Finally, crying out at the pain of his various injuries, he crash-landed on the table. The overturned metal chair was now within reach. He grabbed it, hauled himself to his feet, then swung it wildly at the glass sliding door. A resounding crack was followed by a brief pause, as if the molecules in the glass were debating collectively what to do next. Then the whole door splintered into a spiderweb. Another couple of swings of the chair, and Raffi had made a hole large enough to jump through. Once on the balcony, he sprang onto his hoverbike, started it up and quickly steered it back through the glass door, punching a bigger hole in the glass in the process. He pulled up briefly to check out the situation on the bed. Michael was now sitting up on the bedhead, back to the wall, hemmed in by three lethal menials. His lower trousers and shoes were ripped to bits and his legs and hands were covered in cuts. Raffi took aim, then opened the throttle very slightly. The bike surged forwards, its prow smashing into the blender, which then careened into the mincer, sending both tumbling off the bed. He slammed on the airbrake just before he hit the wall.

'There is nothing wrong with me! There is no need to call the Tech Centre!' screeched Brigitte.

'Get on,' yelled Raffi, but he hardly needed to say it. As soon as he felt the weight of his passenger behind him, Raffi executed a tight turn and shot back through the hole in the glass. He circled for a few moments around the Upper Atrium. Since Brigitte had begun her assault, he'd been living from second to second on adrenaline-fuelled instinct. Now they had escaped he had to start thinking more strategically. His passenger's very existence suddenly made everything non-viable. It was like meeting one's antimatter equivalent: they simply couldn't coexist. He and Michael would have to have a serious talk – figure out what they were going to do next.

He landed on the Mezzanine, near Castafiore's Coffeebar. They attracted the odd stare as Raffi helped Michael off the bike, but not as many as might have been expected, given their physical state. An odd feature of the Chronosphere that Raffi had sometimes wondered about was a lack of concern or even curiosity about strangers. Was it a reflection on the types who entered the Sphere, or just something that happened to people once they were in here? Either way, he was grateful for it right now. They found a spare table outside Castafiore's and Raffi ordered them each a sherbet milkfizz.

'I'm sorry,' he said to the still dazed and speechless Michael. 'I needed a new identity. I wasn't planning on keeping it long – just while I was in here. I didn't realise you'd be coming back.'

Michael coughed and examined the cuts on his hands. 'I should have known something was up,' he said with a pained expression. 'When I came back in, yeah? Reception hadn't realised I'd left.'

'They hacked into the computer, the people who gave me your biometrics,' explained Raffi. 'They changed the records to show you were still here. Like I say, I'm sorry.'

'I suppose it was also you who's been spending my money?'

'I know you won't believe me but I was planning to pay back every u-doll. I just can't use my own bank account at the moment, for obvious reasons.'

Michael looked at him for the first time since their escape. 'I believe you,' he said. 'It would have suited you to let B kill me just now. But you came back for me. That makes what you say now more credible.'

A metallic buzzing suddenly filled the air. It sounded urgent, out of control, like a giant, wounded insect. Raffi jerked his head upwards in dread, half expecting to see one of Brigitte's kitchen gadgets hurtling through the air towards them. Instead he saw a hoverbike careering around above the Mezzanine, then plunging, prow first, into the central fountain. There was a huge splash. A few seconds later a soaking figure, dressed in shorts and a gym vest, staggered out from the shallow pool. Raffi had no trouble recognizing him. He ran up. 'Dario! Are you okay?'

'Just dandy, mate,' beamed Dario, before collapsing to his knees.

'What in hooly happened to you?' asked Raffi, helping him back to his feet. He looked almost worse than Michael – covered in cuts and bruises.

A small crowd had gathered around the fountain, muttering softly, gesturing at Dario and the steaming wreckage of the bike.

'Bloody Christo Ellis showed up,' grimaced Dario. 'As in the real Christo Ellis! Talk about the poo hitting the flipping blower! All bloody hell broke loose. I had Mandy threatening to call the 'thorities. Meanwhile this bloke was basically trying to tear me to shreds as I sat there. I'd only just got up – otherwise I might have given a better account of myself. Of course Mandy locked down the dom, so I had to use a barbell to smash my way out of there. The bastard landed a ferocious pinger on my bike with a broken-off chairleg just as I was taking off – turned my air intake into something sounding like a buzzsaw with laryngitis. Lost all power. Best I could do was steer myself into the waterspout and hope for the best.'

Once they'd seen that Dario was okay and wasn't about to expire, the crowd began to disperse. One, however, remained. 'So *you* stole Christo's identity?' demanded Michael coldly. He was leaning against a bench for support, but continued to stand, despite the obvious pain he was in.

'Who's this?' Dario asked, looking at Raffi.

'The real Michael Storm.'

'Jeebus!'

'Exactly. Come and join us for a milkfizz. We've got some decisions to make.'

'I don't envy you,' said Michael to Dario a little later. 'Christo's a beautiful guy – I should know, we've been together for more than three years – but he's a brute when someone crosses him. He won't stop coming after you. Not ever.'

Dario raised his eyes roofwards. 'Septimus Watts! Of all the people you could have turned me into, you had to choose a gay, homicidal maniac!'

'So what's the plan?' asked Raffi.

'You can keep my Chronospheric identity if you want,' offered Michael. 'I'm getting the hell out of here. When the MAID starts trying to turn you into pork fritters in front of your eyes, you know you've outstayed your welcome. Get your mate to hack back into the computer once I've left, yeah? – and delete the record of my departure, then everything'll be as it was. And if you can give me your bank details, I can make sure that what you spend on my account while you're in here gets refunded…' – he grinned at Raffi – '…just in case – just in case you never make it out of here to pay me back.'

'Of course,' said Raffi.

'That just leaves me,' said Dario. 'Can you speak to that lover-boy rottweiler of yours? Try and sweet-talk him into the idea of leaving, too?'

'I'll do my best,' said Michael. 'I don't want to leave here without him anyways, or we'll get out of sync, right?'

He spoke a number into his wearable, and waited. 'Chrissy. Hi, love… What's the matter? No! Identity thief? I can't believe it… You didn't! That must have been… Yeah, I saw him crash into the fountain a few minutes ago… Dead, yeah! No one could have survived that one… Course I'm sure. There was blood and everything… Listen, Chris, I have to leave again, yeah? I know, I'm sorry, love. The money didn't come through to my account. I'll have to go out and sort things out with the bank. Can you meet me at Temp-Al Four in twenty minutes? Okay?… Love you. Bye.' Click. 'Sorted,' he said to the other two. 'We'll be out of your hair in half an hour.'

He stood and offered his hand to Raffi. Before he could take it, a purple light fell on Michael's face. A huge, maroon-coloured hoverbike descended to their table and a scarlet-leathered arm reached out and snatched the com-stud from Michael's collar. Red Oakes then backed off, floating a metre or so off the ground, grinning like he'd just swallowed half a bottle of his girlfriend's happy pills. 'Redial last number,' he said into the wearable, not taking his laughing eyes off Raffi and Dario. 'Christo Ellis? Sorry to have to say it, but Michael's a big fat liar.'

'No!' said Michael. He tried desperately to grab the stud from Red, but the cyborg deftly reversed out of reach.

'Dario Brice survived his fall into the fountain,' smirked Red, 'and he and your boyfriend are sitting here together at Castafiore's on the Mezzanine having a milkfizz with a chap called Raffi Delgado, who, by the way, tried to steal Michael's ID. Just thought you'd want to know. Tootlepip.'

'You bastard,' roared Dario. He charged into Red's flank and sent his bike into a mad, swaying dance around the cafe, knocking over two waiter droids like a pair of skittles and overturning food plates and coffee cups. In an explosion of broken glass, Red's bike then fell through the café window and landed on its side, discharging the rider.

There were screams from customers and a mass abandonment of coffees, pastries and sorbets as people made for the exits.

Dario's intervention had been spectacular, but – Raffi reckoned – probably too late. Even now, Christo would be descending towards them like an avenging angel from the 120th floor.

'Quick!' Raffi yelled to Dario. 'Grab Red's bike. I'll take Michael on mine. We have to get out of here.'

Dario raced to the fallen bike and was just heaving it back to vertical when Red shoulder-barged him from behind, sending him and the bike tumbling over. Red lifted Dario as if he were made of straw, and pitched him back through the broken café window where he landed on top of a droid which was mopping up the spilled beverage. Dario and droid went skidding along the wet floor and crashed into the bar. Sauces, condiments, paper towels and cutlery rained down on them. The droid was now a broken-necked doll, lolling moronically with a blob of ketchup rolling down its cheek and a pile of napkins for a hat. Dario didn't look much cleverer as he sat semi-stupefied, his orange singlet smeared with coffee and mayonnaise.

Raffi, hovering just outside the café, watched as Red climbed back through the broken window and closed in once more on the helpless Dario. Angrily, Raffi gave it some throttle and sent his bike hurtling through the smashed pane. The prow caught the cyborg squarely between the shoulder blades just as he was reaching for Dario. Red went crashing head first into the wooden bar, splintering the wood as if it was balsa and burying himself up to his waist in cups, plates and glasses, so that little more than his short, heavily muscled legs were left on show. Determined as he was to save Dario and hit back at Red, Raffi hadn't really thought through the consequences of a speeding charge into a modest-sized coffeebar. Far too late he rammed the altimode toggle forwards, trying to gain some height before he, too, came a cropper. The bike rose sufficiently to miss the bar, but crashed at full tilt into the mirror behind, shattering the glass and causing an impressive array of multi-hued bottles to cascade deafeningly to the floor. The bike skidded upwards, looped back on itself and then plummeted heavily to the floor – so that, for Raffi, the world turned briefly upside down before the floor-like sky came crashing down on his head.

He found himself lying in a huge puddle of strong-smelling liquid amid thousands of tiny glass fragments, which covered his hair and clothes. Ever so carefully, he climbed to his feet, avoiding the fizzing remains of the crushed bar droid, and surveyed the wreckage of the café. Through the broken window pane he saw Michael and, confronting him, a huge, muscular guy with a blond buzz cut, clad in black and gold. Christo Ellis – it could be no one other – stood well over two metres and looked about as broad as a transradial. His meaty fist had the front of Michael's shirt in its grasp, so that his boyfriend was forced on tiptoes as he stared fearfully up at him. Christo looked sad rather than angry. 'You lied to me, Mikey,' he accused. 'I hope there's a good reason. I hope these creeps were forcing you to say those things, or God help me I'll –'

'Let me go, Chris,' pleaded Michael. 'You're hurting me. Let me go and I'll explain everything.'

Christo opened his hand and Michael staggered backwards. It was then that he noticed the cuts and bruises on Michael's legs and feet.

'What did he do to you?' He turned towards Raffi. 'Let me get him. I'll turn him into mincemeat.'

'It wasn't him who did it,' cried Michael, pulling at Christo's jacket as the blond colossus began climbing through the window. 'It was B, my MAID. She went mad. Raffi got me out of there. If it wasn't for Raffi, I'd –'

'– not be in this mess to start with,' finished Red, who by now had managed to crawl out of the crockery cupboard and stagger back to his feet. 'It's like thanking an arsonist for pulling you out of a building he set on fire. Whichever way you look at it, old chap, Delgado's ruined your life in here and forced you to leave.'

'No one's forcing anyone to leave,' growled Christo, his eyes still locked murderously on Raffi. He completed his climb through the window and kicked aside a fallen chair. Beneath him, Dario groaned. Christo glanced down and gave

Dario a fast and brutal kick in the ribs, making him screech. Raffi used the distraction to quickly duck down behind the bar and arm himself with a broken bottle.

'Leave him!' cried Michael. 'Just leave them both, yeah? Let's just get out of here.'

'They're the ones who're leaving,' grunted Christo. 'This is their doing.'

'Here, here,' applauded Red, who looked to be having the time of his life.

Raffi tried to back away as Christo reached across the bar towards him, but he underestimated the giant's reach. Christo's fist closed around his throat. Raffi felt himself start to choke as he was lifted clear off his feet and dragged back over the counter top. He smashed the bottle against the side of Christo's fuzzy blond head. The man-mountain merely blinked, then smiled and carried on with what he was doing, which was throttling the life out of his victim. Raffi kicked, punched and clawed at his assailant as he fought for breath. He could feel his lungs straining, his vision and his thoughts blurring. 'Stay alive,' Raffi told himself. 'Just try and stay alive.'

CHAPTER TWENTY-SEVEN

⧗

WORSE THAN DEATH

Everything was going a kind of pearly white, not to mention grey and cloudy, like a wet day in paradise. He could hear his own choking sobs and watch his feeble movements as though he was someone else, floating just a little bit above and to the right. He felt the pain in his throat and lungs, but it was someone else's pain by now. A kind of peace came over him and he knew he must be near the end. Beyond himself, he could see the others. There was Christo, face tight with a hatred that must have its roots in injuries borne far from here and long ago. To his left was Michael silently shouting at him – for earthly sounds were no longer reaching Raffi. To Christo's right was Dario, dear sweet friend, now back on his feet, trying desperately to prise Christo's hand from its throat-grip. Behind them was Red, smiling serenely, looking calmer and less boggle-eyed than Raffi could ever remember. And behind Red, unknown to anyone yet, except for Raffi, or this being Raffi had become, were two black-clad chrono-sans touching down on the

Mezzanine astride their huge bikes. He watched them march into Castafiore's and take aim with their fancy big guns. One of them shouted something, and everyone turned and scattered, except for Christo. The gun emitted a shimmering cone of air and the goliath froze in its beam. Raffi saw himself drop like a heavy sack from the now motionless fist and collapse to the floor. With a tug of sadness, he felt himself drifting back towards the fallen body. It wasn't gravity acting on him, nor magnetism, nor any other known physical force – just an irresistible sense of belonging. And then the pearliness dissolved, the earthly clatter returned and he was looking upwards, coughing his guts out, consumed again by the pain in his upper chest and throat.

Through a forest of legs – both human and chair – he saw Red escaping through the broken window. Before the chrono-sans could react, the cyborg came riding back in through the doorway on his big maroon racer and mowed straight into them. The officers went down, their dilator guns sent flying. With his bionically enhanced reflexes, Red grabbed one in mid-air, switched the dial to zero, and fired it at Christo. The giant roared, flexed his muscles and stampeded towards the fallen police officers, kicking the remaining gun from the armed one's grasp. The chrono-sans backed away, but not before he grabbed them, one in each hand, and flung them through the doorway. They collided with the outdoor furniture, scattering it, before coming to rest close to the fountain.

Only then did Christo's mighty form start to wobble. For a moment it looked as though the temporal whiplash would fell him. Then his eyes lit on half a glass of Alligator coolfizz on one of the tables. He downed it in one, belched and turned back to face the others. 'Now,' he whispered, fixing Raffi once more in his sights. 'Where were we?'

'Right here,' yelled Dario, picking up the fallen dilator and turning it on Christo. He fired. At the same moment, Red, still hovering above the bar on his bike, also opened fire. His beam filled the space that Dario's had to cross to reach its target. The two beams converged, creating a blinding yellow glow in the middle of the room, shot through with bright white sparks. This was accompanied by a loud, jerky buzzing that reminded Raffi of static interference. Christo, caught almost in the middle of this convergence, began to glow himself. When the light and the buzz finally faded, Christo was gone.

'What in hooly was that?' Dario managed to gasp.

'The meeting point of two time speeds – that's always going to be messy.' Dario and Raffi both turned at the sound of the familiar voice.

'Jonah!' cried Dario. Raffi could only smile, too weak as yet to say anything. Despite their semi-estrangement, he couldn't help a surge of happiness at the sight of his friend.

Looking pathetically small and fragile compared to the behemoth he had replaced, Jonah stood at the broken window, appearing amused by the carnage within. 'I heard all the commotion below and I just knew you two had to have something to do with it!'

'Where did my Chrissy go?' asked Michael.

'Precisely!' demanded Red. 'Where is he?'

'Wherever he is, we're better off without him,' croaked Raffi, sitting up and tenderly rubbing his throat.

'Getting caught between timespeeds can't be good,' speculated Jonah. 'The chances are he's dead.'

Michael's head bowed and his knees buckled. 'No! I can't believe it.'

'Your friend ain't dead, he's drifting.'

They all looked up to see one of the chrono-sans gingerly rising to his feet and limping towards them. He glared at Red, who was looking a lot less self-assured now his super-charged ally was no longer around. 'You're in trouble, son. Assaulting a chrono-san is a serious charge. We've got back-up on the way, and they'll be taking you in.'

'I hope they do,' said Red cockily. 'There's a serious case of fraud going on here, which Christo and I were quite capably sorting out before you two blundered in. But don't worry, I'll gladly explain everything to Secrocon, and then those two imposters can be evicted.' He pointed at Dario and Raffi with his dilator.

'Give me that,' demanded the chrono-san, 'or you'll be in even more trouble.'

Red handed it over.

'How do you know he's drifting?' asked Jonah.

'Cos these babies ain't dilators,' explained the chrono-san, running his finger along the gun's muzzle. 'Well, they got a dilator function as you saw just now. But they're actually muftis – multi-functional time-distorters. Got all sorts of tricks, they have – some we don't even properly understand ourselves yet. See, they're a very recent bit of kit. Imagine a dilator, desynchronizer and temp-fi-er all rolled into one.'

'A temp what?'

'Temp Fi-Er stands for temporal field eraser,' said the other chrono-san, who had by now rejoined his colleague. 'They delete people in time as well as space. Once hit by one of those, you're not only dead – it's as if you never lived. Pretty scary actually – hope we never have cause to use that one.' He felt his back and grimaced. 'I'm Chrono-San Lin Croppo, by the way. This is Ference Gearing.

'We're very relieved you showed up,' said Raffi.

'Looks like you had your mufti set to "desync", as I thought,' said Gearing, checking the controls on the top surface of the gun Red had used. 'Normally that would have sent him back or forwards in time. But the crossfire with the other gun changed things. My guess is that he's now flying around in time like an out-of-control hoverbike.'

'Like a fly with a sugar rush,' chuckled Lin Croppo.

'Yeah, but hardly a fly, though Lin,' said his partner, 'rememberin' the size of him.'

'Okay then, like an elephant with a sugar rush.'

''Cept elephants wouldn't get a sugar rush would they?' pointed out Gearing. 'Cos they don't eat sugar.'

'You sure about that?'

'Pretty sure, yeah.'

There was a roar from below and a squadron of six police bikes rose up through the hole at the centre of the Mezzanine like a swarm of huge black wasps. They set down outside Castafiore's and dismounted.

The leader, a big guy with blue epaulettes, entered first through the wrecked doorway. 'Okay Ferry, Croppo. What's going on? Looks like there's been a party.'

'Mornin' Chrono-Don Moodle. Quite a party, yeah.'

As Gearing gave his report, Raffi began hearing an intermittent buzzing nearby, similar to the sound earlier when the mufti beams had crossed. Suddenly, Christo reappeared in the room – or a slightly flickery version of him, like a sensovision with a poor broadcast signal. The giant swiftly solidified, looking madder than ever. Growling, he swung his fists, one of which connected with Chrono-Don Moodle's chin and the other with Ference Gearing's arm, sending his gun spinning across the floor in Red's direction.

As the great blond bear advanced on the line of chrono-sans, they nervously raised their weapons. But before they could fire, he flickered, then vanished – careering away like an astronaut with a faulty thruster to some other random point in time.

'Was that him?' gurgled the captain, spitting blood.

'Yuh,' replied Lin. 'Cross-beamed by two muftis set to desync. Hell knows if we'll ever see him again, or keep him here long enough to trap him.'

'Well, try!' Moodle turned to the rest of the squad. 'All of you, set your guns to resync and keep 'em trained on the spot where he disappeared. When you see him, blast him.' Then he checked out Red. Gearing's gun was no longer on the floor, but it wasn't back in the officer's hand either. To tell by the smirk on the cyborg's face, Raffi guessed it had found its way into Red's pocket.

'You!' Moodle pointed at him. 'Get off your bike. You're coming back to the Police Centre with me.' Moodle signalled to two of the squad. One of them trained his gun on Red while the other tried to manhandle the young man off his bike. But Red brushed the chrono-san aside and dismounted himself. The three then followed the captain out of the bar.

The scratchy buzzing began again as they approached their bikes. This time Christo appeared outside the coffeebar. Like an oversized barrel of fury, he erupted into existence with a roar that started quiet and quickly grew deafening. He ran at the line of police bikes so they all toppled like dominoes. Then he lowered his head and charged at the captain and his sidekicks. Red's reflexes saved him once again and he ducked out of the way while the other three felt the full force of Christo's uncontained ferocity and were knocked clean out of their conscious minds. The remaining five officers had all been facing the wrong way. Surprised and frightened, they turned, raised their guns and fired, but the beams bounced harmlessly off the heavy rectangular coffeebar table that Christo was now holding before him as a shield. The shield swiftly became a weapon as Christo charged at the window, breaking the last of its glass and very nearly Jonah's skull. For once grateful to be small and easily overlooked, Jonah dodged out of the way and darted further into the shadows of the room. Christo then threw the table hard at the chrono-sans, catching them full in the face with the heavy wooden surface.

'Here, Christo. You may want this, old boy.' The giant turned and caught the gun tossed to him by Red. 'I've set it to Temp Fi-Er,' grinned the cyborg.

'No!' cried Jonah, leaping up. 'That's… that's worse than death!'

'Good,' chuckled Christo. 'I like the sound of that.' He stepped through what remained of the window and placed his boots down hard on the upturned table, forcing a groan from the stunned chrono-sans lying beneath it. Standing there on the table, Christo once again fixed on Raffi. 'I'm not done with you, mister!' he cried, raising the gun and taking aim.

Raffi, still weakened from injury, was in no position to defend himself. His one remaining hope was that time might whisk his would-be killer away on another brisk journey to 'elsewhen'. But Christo was looking solid, at least for now. Raffi closed his eyes, shutting out the sight of that ferocious red face above the gun barrel. Worse than death, Jonah had called it. Non-existence. It would be like you hadn't lived at all. The people who knew you, loved you – so it would turn out – never actually did. The last thing he saw before the golden fire flew out towards him – and this surprised him, for he hadn't thought of her in a while – was his mother, Maria Delgado, looking proudly at him, as she had on the morning he'd left. There she stood in the doorway of their domicile, smiling, haloed in that golden light.

⧗

CHAPTER TWENTY-EIGHT

THE WORLD AS HE FOUND IT

hadow. A shadow eclipsed the light just as it was about to embrace him. The light enclosed the shadow like a shimmering web. The shadow was solid. Human.

Michael.

Then it was gone.

Before him, amid the wreckage of the Castafiore Coffeebar, was Christo Ellis, on his knees, groping at the space his boyfriend Michael had once occupied. Christo clawed uselessly at the specks of dust that glinted in the afternoon light now pouring in from the Upper Atrium of Time Tower. His face was in the shape of a scream, his eyes desolate.

'Where is he? Where's Mikey gone?'

'He leapt in front of the temp-fi-er beam,' said Jonah. 'He saved Raffi's life.'

'Just like Raffi saved his,' said Dario.

'Will – will he come back?'

'No,' said Jonah. 'But soon the pain will go.' Hesitantly he placed a hand on Christo's heaving shoulder. 'Soon you won't remember anything about him.'

'I–I don't want to forget him,' roared Christo. 'I don't want the pain to go.'

He pushed the weapon's muzzle into his chest. 'I want to go there with him.'

'But he's nowhere.'

'Well I want to be nowhere, too.'

He pulled the trigger for the second time and silky golden light like morning mist enfolded his huge, sobbing form. The light glowed more strongly as the figure within it faded.

The ensuing period was confusing for everyone – Raffi, Jonah, Dario, the chrono-sans, Red – especially Red. Everyone knew that something violent and possibly tragic had taken place in Castafiore's, but for the life of them, no one could remember what. The three 'perpetrators' were called into the Police Centre a couple of days later for questioning by a bruised, not to mention bewildered, Chrono-Don Horatio Moodle.

'Begin at the beginning,' he ordered them. 'How did it all start?'

Raffi explained that as far as he could remember it had begun earlier that morning when Brigitte, his MAID, had malfunctioned – though what had triggered that malfunction he couldn't exactly say. She had become violent – hence the cuts and burns on his feet and legs. He remembered escaping from his dom and then coming to Castafiore's. Shortly afterwards he'd seen Christo crash-landing.

Moodle turned his attention to Dario. 'Christo Ellis. Perhaps you can explain why you crashed into the fountain.

Dario shrugged. 'Sorry, chrono-don. Some heavy shit happened in my dom and I had to get out fast, but I couldn't say what.'

'Was it your MAID?'

'Don't think so. Mandy's cool.'

'Then while we were at the coffeebar, Red showed up,' continued Raffi. 'He was behaving threateningly.'

'And why doesn't that surprise me?' grunted Moodle. 'From what I've seen of you, young man, a spell in Re-Ed wouldn't go amiss.'

'Damn it all,' said Red, rubbing his brow in an effort to think. 'I had something on these two, chrono-don. I just wish I could remember what it was. For months I've been telling anyone who'd listen, and plenty who wouldn't, that they're not Storm and Ellis – they're the fugitives Delgado and Brice. If only people would use their eyes like I do, but you officials are so obsessed with biometrics you're losing the ability to see what's in front of your noses.'

'I'm aware of your views, Mr Oakes,' sighed Moodle. 'I checked your file earlier and I see you've made no less than five formal accusations of this nature to five different officers. But we're not here to discuss your views on the identity of these two young men. We're here to work out what the hell happened yesterday morning at Castafiore's. Now do you or do you not remember what you said or did when you arrived there?'

Red shook his head miserably. 'All I know is that Brice here gave my bike a shove and sent me crashing through the window.'

'You mean Mr Ellis?'

'Whatever,' he shrugged.

'And then?'

'Then Brice was making to steal my bike, so I grabbed him and threw him back through the same window. I was about to go in and give him a good thrashing when Delgado catches me in the back at full tilt on his bike, sends me head first into the pots and pans.'

'So far just a typical lads' brawl then. What next?' Moodle stared at the three young faces.

'That's where it starts getting a little confusing,' said Raffi. 'I think… there were others there by then.'

'I got a vicious kick from somewhere,' Dario offered.

'And I got a horrific neck lock or something. I couldn't breathe – might have died if your men hadn't shown up – Officers Croppo and Gearing.'

'Fine men, both of them,' nodded Moodle. 'And completely useless witnesses. About as bad as you lot.'

'Anyway, they got caught up in the fight. I think Red rode into them at one stage, but I can't be sure.'

'A total lie,' declared Red.

Moodle stared at the three of them for a long time. Then stood up. 'You're lucky this time, boys,' he said. 'There are too many blanks in this story to make any sense of it, so we won't be taking further action. But you will have to pay a fine to compensate the coffeebar owners for the damage. I would say a third each is fair, wouldn't you?'

No one complained. Raffi, who had stayed at Dario's the night before, returned to his domicile later that day with a couple of Tech Support guys. The place was spotless and smelled fresh and clean as Raffi had half suspected it would. Tech Support nevertheless gave Brigitte a thorough overhaul. She behaved impeccably throughout their visit, answering all their questions as fully and cooperatively as anyone could expect. As for the incident two days ago, she wasn't sure what Michael could be referring to exactly. Had she not been her usual cheerful self? If not she sincerely apologised and would try harder in future. She wished to assure him that she would strive to be a model of politeness, helpfulness and good companionship from this day forward. It was an impressive performance, and Raffi expected no less from the actress he knew her to be. As for the tech guys, they were more than happy to give her a clean bill of health.

But what exactly had happened? As the weeks passed, the memories, such as they were, of that strange day faded, until the whole incident began to take on the quality of a dream. Meanwhile, the Chronosphere continued to deliver on its promise of time – bounteous, abundant oceans of it. Morning, noon and night, day in, day out, week in, week out, Raffi played, competed, raced and partied with the best of them. And for all his nagging fears about the real agenda of the people who ran the place, he understood that he was actually having the time of his life. This was the best thing that had ever happened to him – maybe the best thing that would ever happen to him. This was not a place nor a time for doubt, fear or introspection. The Chronosphere was the cathedral of a new kind of religion, whose creed was pleasure without end – and he resolved to embrace it and worship at its altars like the most pious devotee.

Acknowledgements

These books were partly inspired by the ideas contained in some classic science fiction stories, including H. G. Wells' '*The New Accelerator*', Ian Watson's '*The Very Slow Time Machine*' and Brian Aldiss' '*Man In His Time*'.

I also consulted numerous fascinating and occasionally wacky websites to help me develop theories of time and create a plausible-seeming future. In particular, I would like to acknowledge Peter Lynds for his theories about time and Zeno's paradoxes, Michael Buchanan for his ideas about temporal fields, *The Observer*'s brilliant 'The future of food' feature, and Research Media and Cybernetics for the information on EHD thrusters, upon which the technology of the hoverbikes was loosely based.

On a personal note, I would like to thank my mother and father, my sister Kelly, my nephew Alistair and my brother-in-law Steven for their helpful comments on earlier drafts of this book. I would also like to thank my wife Paola for her unwavering love and support.

ABOUT THE AUTHOR

Alex Woolf was born in Willesden Green, North London. He studied History and Politics at university.

He spent his 20s riding his motorbike, travelling and working, including a brief stint as a dish-washer in a roach-infested restaurant in Florida.

Since 2001, he has been an editor and author of children's books and has written on a wide range of subjects, from spiders to Nazis.

Alex lives in North London with his Italian wife and two children.

Chronosphere: Time out of Time is his debut novel.

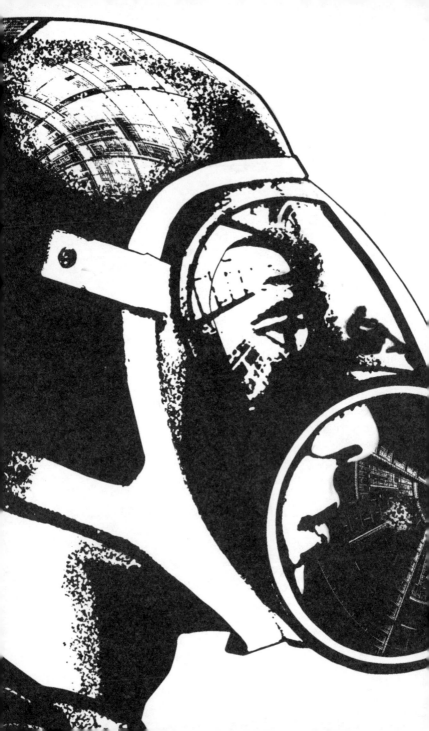

THE ADVENTURE CONTINUES...

CHRONOSPHERE

Book 2

Malfunction

by Alex Woolf

It starts slowly at first, with meals being served cold and food going off, then residents start to notice the blistering heat and haywire android servants. But soon the entire Chronosphere is malfunctioning, causing a complete breakdown of society and the eruption of a fierce turf war between rival gangs.

Caught in the middle of the crossfire are Raffi Delgado and his fellow chrononauts Dario, Sal, Jonah and Lastara. With the help of familiar faces and old enemies, they put into place a brave rescue attempt, but in doing so the dark truth about the source of the Malfunction and the real aims of the Chronomaster become all too clear.

PUBLISHED SEPTEMBER 2011 BY

A division of Book House

The Salariya Book Company is
publisher of books for children
internationally. Through our imp
Scribo we are dedicated to publ
appeal, using innovative concep
informative writing and, above a
of young people. With a mind fo
books are printed on paper from
links below to visit our imprints
Blog or dive into a world of free
best-selling 'You Wouldn't War

Children's
non-fiction
and graphic
novels

Fiction for children and teenagers

www.salariya.com
where books come to life!

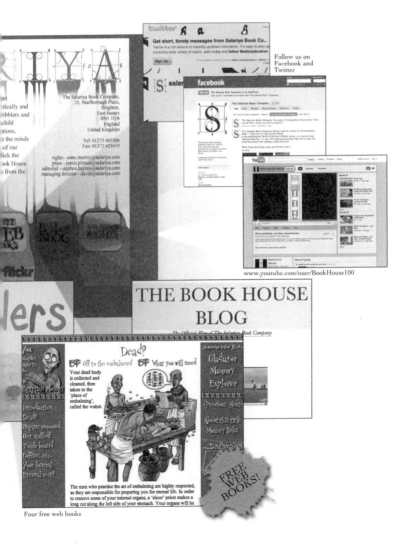

Follow us on Facebook and Twitter

www.youtube.com/user/BookHouse100

THE BOOK HOUSE
BLOG

The Official Blog of The Salariya Book Company

FREE WEB BOOKS!

Four free web books

Cherished Library

Very Peculiar Histories™

Ancient Egypt
Jim Pipe
ISBN: 978-1-906714-92-5

The World Cup
David Arscott
ISBN: 978-1-907184-38-3

London
Jim Pipe
ISBN: 978-1-907184-26-0

The Blitz
David Arscott
ISBN: 978-1-907184-18-5

Christmas
Fiona Macdonald
ISBN: 978-1-907184-50-5

Global Warming
Ian Graham
ISBN: 978-1-907184-51-2

Castles
Jacqueline Morley
ISBN: 978-1-907184-48-2

Rations
David Arscott
ISBN: 978-1-907184-25-3

Vampires
Fiona Macdonald
ISBN: 978-1-907184-39-0